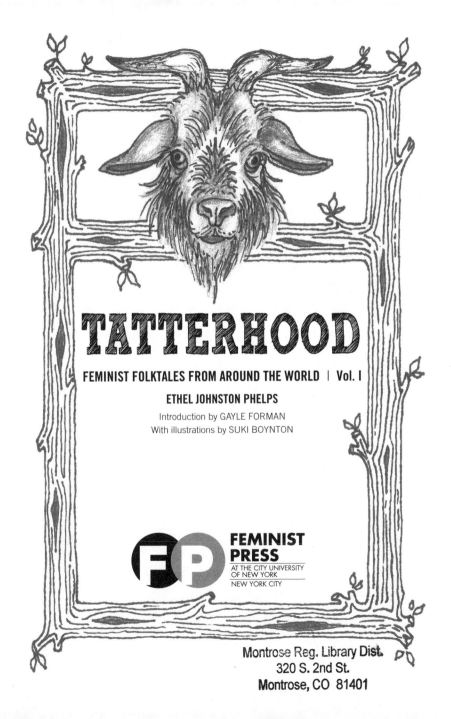

# TATTERHOOD

## FEMINIST FOLKTALES FROM AROUND THE WORLD | Vol. I

### ETHEL JOHNSTON PHELPS

Introduction by GAYLE FORMAN
With illustrations by SUKI BOYNTON

FEMINIST
PRESS
AT THE CITY UNIVERSITY
OF NEW YORK
NEW YORK CITY

Published in 2016 by the Feminist Press
at the City University of New York
The Graduate Center
365 Fifth Avenue, Suite 5406
New York, NY 10016

feministpress.org

First Feminist Press edition 2016

Copyright information continues on page 170

This book was made possible thanks to a grant from New York State Council on the Arts with the support of Governor Andrew Cuomo and the New York State Legislature.

Second printing December 2017

Cover design, text design, and illustrations by Suki Boynton

Library of Congress Cataloging-in-Publication Data is available for this title.

*For Rachael, Jenny, and Nancy,*
*who love tales of magic and adventure*

# CONTENTS

# TATTERHOOD

## FEMINIST FOLKTALES FROM AROUND THE WORLD | Vol. I

# INTRODUCTION
## GAYLE FORMAN

**S**tories matter.

They are among the first things we hear. *Once upon a time*, a parent whispers to a baby. And a story begins.

As children, we swim in stories. We marinate in them. We repeat them, tweak them, weave them into our own developing stories, our own developing identities. We use them to explore adventure, danger, independence, romance. We borrow personas and test-drive personalities—internalizing characters and all their embedded codes of what it means to be a hero, a heroine, a man, a woman, to be rescued, to be a rescuer, to be valued.

Stories matter.

Not long ago, I took my two daughters to see a film adaptation of *Cinderella*, one of the most enduring of stories. It wasn't as if I was expecting much.

But after the recent spate of more feminist-leaning fairy tales to hit the screen, I hadn't expected such a doubling down on the fantasy. Not simply that Prince Charming will save the girl, but that the best course of action for a young woman to take in the face of adversity—even abuse—is to smile, sing a song, and have a pleasantly patient attitude.

I was mortified. *Horrified.* I felt like I'd exposed them to something toxic and insidious. This was not a life lesson I wanted them to emulate. Ever. (For their part, they couldn't believe I was getting so hot and bothered about a *movie*. But I was.) I couldn't believe that still, in 2016—when we had Hillary Clinton running for president, when we had women on college campuses forcing administrations to deal with rape and abuse head-on, when we had Beyoncé and Amy Schumer—this myth still had potency. That it was still a story people would aspire to (and judging by the swooning in the audience when Prince Charming fit Cinderella with her slipper, it was).

But of course it was. The story had the comfort and familiarity of a soft blanket. It was the same story that girls and women have been told for decades. That a happy ending is something bestowed—not achieved—and best acquired by waiting, patiently, preferably with a sweet song.

There are not many sweet songs in the stories in *Tatterhood*. What there is in these stories is a lot of heart and moxie, cunning and courage, humor and humanity. Consider Tatterhood, a "raggedy" young woman who expends little energy caring about her appearance ("I will go as I am," she laughs when offered a pretty dress) because she is far too busy outsmarting trolls and commandeering ships and saving sisters. Or the delightfully irreverent women in "What Happened to Six Wives Who Ate Onions," who, having grown tired of their husbands' complaints about their off-putting breath, ditch the whiners to climb into the sky and become stars. Or Maru-me and her mother and grandmother in "Three Strong Women," who humble the mightiest wrestler and teach him true strength. Or . . . I could list them all.

Taken in concert, the heroines in *Tatterhood* raise the bar on what it means to be heroic, setting the bar where most girls can touch it. Because in these stories, girls might actually see themselves. Who they are. And who they dream of becoming.

Stories matter.

They matter because they give us mirrors and windows.

When a girl reads or sees one of those stale, sexist, confining, traditional fairy tales, will the image reflected back at her come close to the girl she is? Probably not. It may even distort who she is, or subtly disparage the woman she yearns to be.

But in this wonderful, witty collection, the mirror shines on dozens of glittering images, reflecting and reinforcing the myriad ways there are to be brave, to be kind, to be strong, to be beautiful, to be a savior, to be a heroine, to be a girl, and to be a boy. And best yet, these reflections actually resemble the readers themselves. The stories in *Tatterhood* have been culled from folktales around the world; they include, among others, Sudanese, Native American, Scottish, Irish, and Japanese tales. Which means the characters within them reflect both the diversity of girlhood and the diversity of humanity.

And that matters. It matters a lot.

A few months after I saw *Cinderella*, I started reading *Tatterhood* while waiting for my youngest daughter to finish up a hip-hop class. Next to me a boy, about ten, looked over and said: "Oh, I love that book."

"This one?" I asked, pointing to a young adult novel about teens and police brutality that I'd been reading earlier.

"No, that one." He pointed to *Tatterhood*. "My mom read it to me."

I'd just started it so I asked him which story he liked best.

"The one with the lady and the elephant," he replied immediately.

"'Unanana and the Elephant'?" I said. I'd read that one, about Unanana, the mother who manages to free her children after they are swallowed whole by an elephant. We discussed how Unanana found the elephant, giving her bonus points for cooking the pot of beans beforehand so she could feed her hungry children from inside its belly. Because beans were so satisfying that way, we agreed.

As we discussed the book, I realized how I'd underestimated not only the boy (why wouldn't he like a book just because the stories highlight female heroes?), but the power of the story itself. It was a clarifying reminder that this collection provided windows and mirrors for boys too. To see themselves as perhaps they might like to be—equitable partners, worthy helpmates, and sometimes the beneficiary of a good rescue—and to see girls depicted not as damsels in distress but as the strong capable people they know them to be.

Stories matter.

For the realities they reflect and the aspirations they illuminate. For boys and for girls. For women and for men. They matter because after tens of thousands of years, they are still the way we explain who we are, and who we want to be.

Who do we want to be? Who do we want our daughters to be? And our sons?

Think about that. And tell the story.

# PREFACE
## ETHEL JOHNSTON PHELPS

The tales in this book are old stories about magic and adventure. They are stories that ordinary people in the past told to entertain their families and friends. The stories were not originally thought of as "children's tales," but generations of children have loved hearing them.

The people in these tales do not behave the way girls and boys, women and men, have usually been expected to behave in real life and in stories. The heroes are not superior; they are human and vulnerable. The heroines have energy, wit, and sense.

Many of these tales are over a thousand years old, and they have been continually retold—usually by women. Each generation of womenfolk passed on its stories to succeeding generations. In publishing these tales, retold again for today's young people, the Feminist Press is one more link in this chain of women storytellers.

The stories in this book were chosen for a special characteristic that singles them out from other folk and fairy tales.[1] They portray active and courageous girls and women in the leading roles. The protagonists are heroines in the true and original meaning of the word—heroic women distinguished by extraordinary courage and achievements, who hold the center of interest in the tales.

Active heroines are not common among the folktales that survived by finding their way into print; and it is the printed survivals that are the main sources of the tales we know today. Since these tales come from the body of folktale literature that began to be translated into English in the nineteenth century, they reflect a Western European bias. It is therefore not possible to say that the observations made here apply to all folk literature, but only to the published tales we have inherited.

The overwhelming majority of these tales present males as heroes, with girls and women in minor or subservient roles; or they feature young women like Cinderella and Sleeping Beauty, who pas-

1. The term *fairy tale* is often used to refer to folktales especially for children; to distinguish folktales dealing with supernatural elements; to signify a tale revised or created by a known author. *Fairy tale* and *folktale* are also used interchangeably. Since all the tales in this book are genuine folktales, I have chosen to use that term.

sively await their fate. Only rarely, scattered among the surviving tales, do we find stories of girls and women who are truly heroines, who take the leading part and solve the problems posed by the adventure. It must be remembered, of course, that out of the enormous literature of oral folktales, including every culture around the globe and reaching back well over a thousand years, many tales were lost during the centuries of verbal transmission. What proportion of these "lost" tales might have featured active heroines can only be a matter of conjecture.

The awakening nationalism of the nineteenth century brought a sudden surge of interest in the oral tales of the common people. Their tales were seen as a vanishing national heritage that should be collected and preserved. The Grimm brothers began this task with the publication of *Nursery and Household Tales* in 1812; other European and British scholars soon followed.

Only a few women published collections of local tales in the nineteenth century. Almost all the folktale collectors of the period were well-educated males of a different social class from the rural storytellers they solicited. For Europeans collecting in Asia and Africa, the factor of race would be an additional impediment to securing truly representative tales.

Folklorists Andrew Lang, George W. Dasent, and Stith Thompson, for example, wrote of the difficulties all folklorists experienced in collecting tales. Although women, particularly elderly women, were "the repositories of these national treasures" (a nation's folktales) and the best sources of fairy and supernatural tales, some rural women were reported as unwilling to divulge their store of tales to the collector, for fear of ridicule. These reports referred to various areas of Europe, but the same note is made by Sarah F. Bourhill and Beatrice L. Drake, who published tales gathered in South Africa around the turn of the century. Among black South Africans, they noted, women were most often the village storytellers; however, the women told Bourhill and Drake that they feared ridicule if they told their tales to whites.[2]

Many women did, of course, recite their tales to collectors. But the reticence of some suggests, at the very least, that the tales they were willing to recite were probably those they felt would be socially acceptable and pleasing to the collector. Taking such factors into account, it seems likely that although the preservation and oral transmission of folktales had for centuries been shared by rural women and

2. *Fairy Tales from South Africa*, London, 1908, Introduction, p. v.

men, a much smaller proportion of the tales women knew were collected, recorded, and published. The scarcity of heroic women and girls in the folktales available today may be one consequence.

Nevertheless, women have always been deeply involved in preserving and transmitting this body of marvelously imaginative folk material. They enjoyed and retold the tales while working or at leisure. Their repertory was often large, and they performed with skill as storytellers, passing on the tales to succeeding generations of women. The phrase "old wives' tales," now used derisively, takes on a new and more positive meaning—for the old wives' tales were, indeed, the very rich and varied source of each nation's heritage of folk literature.

A few folktales were published in the eighteenth century specifically for children, but it was not until the latter half of the nineteenth century that the tales definitively became a part of children's literature. Andrew Lang's many volumes of fairy tales attained great popularity. It is worth noting, that although Andrew Lang selected the stories, it was Leonora Blanche Alleyne Lang, his wife, who translated, adapted, and retold for young readers the bulk of the collection, which eventually ran to over three hundred stories. Young women relatives and friends contributed the remaining tales. At the end of the preface to each of the books, Andrew Lang made specific acknowledgment of all these contributions. "My part," he wrote, "has been that of Adam . . . in the garden of Eden. Eve worked, Adam superintended. I also superintend. . . . I find out where the stories are and advise."[3] However, Andrew Lang never saw fit to include his wife's name on the title page along with his own.

The Lang fairy tale books, like all collections of this kind, were retold tales, as are the tales in this collection. Adult readers are sometimes troubled by the retelling of folktales, feeling that they should not be "tampered with." But which version of a tale is authentic, and what is meant by "tampering" is not altogether clear.

In fact, the one thing that is certain about traditional folktales is that they have been constantly retold, with new tellers changing details and emphasis to suit both the time and the local audience. Most of the tales exist in many versions or variants, often appearing in different countries, sometimes in different areas of one country. There is no one "authentic" version of a folktale.

While the stories in this collection are retold stories, they are all traditional folktales. In editing and,

3. Andrew Lang, *The Lilac Fairy Book*, London, 1910, Preface, p. vii.

in some cases, retelling these tales, my general purpose has been to sharpen and illuminate the basic story for the greater enjoyment of children today. Since the evocation of a faraway time and place is a large part of a tale's power to charm, I have kept to the style of the sources and retained much of their language, including old and obsolete words. In some stories, I have changed certain minor external details, but plot and characters are unaltered. Elements of violence or cruelty that serve no purpose intrinsic to the tale, however, have been omitted or moderated; similarly with unnecessary emphasis on remarkable physical beauty.

In the distant past, the art of storytelling was a major source of community and family entertainment, and the tales were used and perceived in certain ways not central to present-day needs. Then as now, they offered a temporary escape from reality into the realm of fancy, distracting the mind and stimulating the imagination. Sometimes the tales served to explain or rationalize the terrors of the inexplicable and the unknown physical world. Because their themes echoed the accumulated experiences and beliefs of a people's past, they were capsules of folk wisdom, teaching and redefining moral and social values. Promoting messages by implication, rather than by obvious moralizing, they provided food for thought and discussion.

Encounters with the supernatural usually provide the action in these adventure tales. But whether the plot deals with supernatural creatures or humans, the problems posed test the character of the protagonists. Even though magic or wise advice may help them, it is their heroic qualities of courage or compassion, or their pluck or daring or wit, that enable them to successfully combat the varied forces of "evil." These forces may be greater or lesser. Characteristically, folktales imply that goodness will triumph over "evil."

Although the positive traits displayed by the successful protagonist still have meaning today, it is apparent that the social customs in the old tales, as well as some of their values, are outdated. How is it, then, that they continue to attract and entertain a contemporary audience? One answer is that a good adventure story dealing with the supernatural will always find an audience. The taste for adventures with the irrational and unknown, as well as the need for escape from reality, has not declined, but seems to fulfill a universal need in both adults and children. And in the underlying themes of the tales we find a comment on personal and social questions that still concern us: how couples conduct their relationships, how old women face threatening circumstances, how young men and women set about solving dilemmas perplexing to themselves or to the community. Although the themes are played out in a realm of magic spells, giants, fairies, and hobgoblins, the imaginative experience can be the yeast of creative thought that carries over to a more prosaic world. This, too, may be among the reasons that folktales are one of the few forms of children's stories enjoyed by "children of all ages."

Folktales also serve to provide a continuing link with the past, both in the sense of a heritage shared with many, and as a part of the individual's personal past—for it is usually the adult who enjoyed folktales as a child who is eager to pass on to children the same enjoyment.

The emotional satisfaction children derive from the tales arises not only from the protagonist's achievement of success or good fortune against odds, but in seeing justice meted out to evildoers—as it often is to children themselves when they misbehave. Reassured by the traditional happy endings of fairy tales, children can delight in the perilous adventures.

Not all the tales that survive today exemplify the merits just discussed, nor do they meet with the wholehearted approval of parents and teachers.

Cruelty and violence in the tales have been a subject of concern for some time. More recently, feminists have criticized the tales for their overemphasis on physical attractiveness, as well as the predominance of female characters who are meek and passive or heartlessly evil.

The danger—or value—of cruelty and violence in children's fiction is, of course, a controversial subject, encompassing television fare and comic books as well as classic literature. Among folktale collectors, the Grimm brothers have been singled out most often for the goriness of their collections. It is useful to remember, however, that folktales were originally shaped for an adult audience, and one that has long since vanished. Many of the descriptive details of folktales reflect the period and the attitudes of the societies from which they sprang. These details are not sacred, nor does their alteration generally affect the basic theme, plot, and characters of the tale. What is important to a tale's meaning is that justice be done unambiguously—a consideration that does not invariably require adopting all of the retributive details of the source. It is not surprising that changed attitudes toward cruel and unusual punishments should influence choices among the tales and the ways in which they are retold, as is the case with the selections in this book.

While feminist critics have raised objections to the convention of the heroine's surpassing beauty, there is no general agreement on this point. Some commentators suggest that the heroine's beauty is not the surface perfection of eyes, complexion, and hair, but the whole beauty of a joyous and radiant person, a symbol of inner beauty, of character and personality. This interpretation of outer beauty, however, is an adult concept that may not be held by the average child; and certainly, for many children, it is discouraging to read that all heroines are extremely beautiful. More important, to be valued primarily for her beauty demeans the other qualities a heroine may possess. Although elements of extraordinary beauty, like those of extraordinary cruelty and violence, are an integral part of some plots, in many tales these are embellishments that can be dropped without affecting the story.

However, while it is possible to revise some elements of folktales without destroying their integrity, the fact remains that the largest number of them portray girls and women unfavorably. We would not want all fictional images of women to be uniformly— and unrealistically—admirable. What is troubling is that although stereotypes of both sexes are common in folktales, there is a marked pervasiveness of older women as frightening hags or evil crones, and of young women and girls as helpless or passive creatures. There are too few surviving tales of likable old women and active, resourceful young women to provide a balanced assortment. In the thirteen tales in this book, you will encounter many characters of women and girls, and only one—the jealous mother of Kate Crackernuts—is a lamentably undesirable character. True, this redresses the balance with sheer force of numbers—but it is a balance that badly needs redressing.

Besides objecting to the folktale conventions mentioned above, some adult readers question the relevance of the omnipresent queens, kings, princes, and princesses to the world of contemporary children. To children, however, as to the country folk who developed the tales, these rulers are symbols of might and wealth. As such, they represent power far beyond a child's command. At the same time, these royal beings move in a fanciful world as easily entered by children as by the rural audience that heard the tales.

For the queens, kings, princes, and princesses of the tales bear little resemblance to any royalty, then or now. Rather, they resemble the well-to-do landowner, farmer, and squire who were in fact the ruling class of the local countryside in Western Europe. Their actions and behavior are those of a prosperous landowner's family. A prince goes to the castle stable to saddle his own horse, a princess hires herself out as a menial servant, another is sent off to buy fresh eggs—and so on. The "kingdoms" are very small, about the size of a village, and a day's walk often brings the protagonist to another "kingdom." This is a world not only within the grasp of the rural tellers—it is a world that a child's limited experience can comprehend.

The society depicted is usually simple; and in this simple, altogether fictional world, peasants and potentates intermingle and converse, moving apparently with little difficulty from one social level to another. Sometimes high rank or riches are achieved through cleverness, sometimes through an advantageous marriage. Whatever the specific device, it is the virtues and abilities of the protagonist that bring the material rewards so often included in the happy ending.

Marriage is also a traditional happy ending, and one that may appear outmoded measured by the standards of adults who wish to promote respect for the status of single persons of both sexes. Such a progressive view has in fact made headway, supported by the economics of an urban society. The tales, on the other hand, came out of the experience of a rural people concerned with problems of survival and the hopes and fears related to it. Marriage brought the establishment of one's own household and the continuity of offspring, conferring a settled place in the social and economic structure— all of which were necessary for rural survival and prosperity in earlier centuries. Thus, marrying and living happily ever afterward symbolizes all the material, social, and personal rewards achieved by the protagonist, whether male or female; to alter it in such cases would be to rob the tale of its meaning. The marriage ending reflects negatively on women in the general run of folktales only because the "heroine" does little except sit, wish, and wait for this goal, with no power over her fate and no active involvement in choosing or planning the circumstances of her future.

The tales in this book describe many different kinds of heroines and heroes, but all the heroines, in one way or another, take on active roles and make decisions to shape their lives. It is this that sets them apart from the static "heroines" customarily found in folktale collections. Out of the few surviving tales that give us true heroines, we have selected a gallery of strong, delightful women and girls for readers of all ages to enjoy.

Once upon a time there was a king and a queen who had no children, and this grieved the queen very much. She was always bewailing their lack of a family and saying how lonesome it was in the palace with no young ones about.

The king remarked that if it were young ones she wanted running about, they could invite the children of their kinswoman to stay with them. The queen thought this a good idea, and soon she had two little nieces romping through the rooms and playing in the palace courtyard.

One day as the queen watched fondly from the window, she saw her two lassies playing ball with a stranger, a little girl clad in tattered clothes. The queen hurried down the stairs.

"Little girl," said the queen sharply, "this is the palace courtyard. You cannot play in here!"

"We asked her in to play with us," cried the lassies, and they ran over to the ragged little girl and took her by the hand.

"You would not chase me away if you knew the powers my mother has," said the strange little girl.

"Who is your mother?" asked the queen, "and what powers does she have?"

The child pointed to a woman selling eggs in the marketplace outside the palace gates. "If she wants to, my mother can tell people how to have children, when all else has failed."

Now this caught the queen's interest at once. She said, "Tell your mother I wish to speak to her in the palace."

The little girl ran out to the marketplace, and it was not long before a tall, strong market woman strode into the queen's sitting room.

"Your daughter says you have powers, and that you could tell me how I may have children of my own," said the queen.

"The queen should not listen to a child's chatter," answered the woman.

"Sit down," said the queen, and she ordered fine food and drinks to be served. Then she told the egg woman she wanted children of her own more than anything in the world. The woman finished her ale, then said cautiously that perhaps she did know a spell it would do no harm to try.

"You must have two pails of water brought to you before you go to bed," said the egg woman. "In each of them you must wash yourself, and afterward, pour away the water under the bed. When you look under the bed the next morning, two flowers will have sprung up: one fair and one rare. The fair one you must eat, but the rare one you must let stand. Mind you, don't forget that."

The queen followed this advice, and the next morning under the bed stood two flowers. One was green and oddly shaped; the other was pink and fragrant. The pink flower she ate at once. It tasted so sweet that she promptly ate the other one as well, saying to herself, "I don't think it can help or hurt either way!"

Not long afterward the queen realized she was with child, and some time later she had the birthing. First was born a girl who had a wooden spoon in her hand and rode upon a goat. A queer looking little creature she was, and the moment she came into the world, she bawled out, "Mama!"

"If I'm your mama," said the queen, "God give me grace to mend my ways!"

"Oh, don't be sorry," said the girl, riding about

on the goat, "the next one born will be much fairer looking." And so it was. The second twin was born fair and sweet, which pleased the queen very much.

The twin sisters were as different as they could be, but they grew up to be very fond of each other. Where one was, the other must be. But the elder twin soon had the nickname "Tatterhood," for she was strong, raucous, and careless, and was always racing about on her goat. Her clothes were always torn and mud-spattered, her hood in tatters. No one could keep her in clean, pretty dresses. She insisted on wearing old clothes, and the queen finally gave up and let her dress as she pleased.

One Christmas Eve, when the twin sisters were almost grown, there arose a terrific noise and clatter in the gallery outside the queen's rooms. Tatterhood asked what it was that dashed and crashed about in the passage. The queen told her it was a pack of trolls who had invaded the palace.

The queen explained that this happened in the palace every seven years. There was nothing to be done about the evil creatures; the palace must all ignore the trolls and endure their mischief.

Tatterhood said, "Nonsense! I will go out and drive them away."

Everyone protested—she must leave the trolls alone; they were too dangerous. But Tatterhood insisted she was not afraid of the trolls. She could and would drive them away. She warned the queen that all doors must be kept shut tight. Then she went out into the gallery to chase them. She laid about with the wooden spoon, whacking trolls on the head or shoulders, rounding them up to drive them out. The whole palace shook with the crashes and shrieking, until it seemed the place would fall apart.

Just then her twin sister, who was worried about Tatterhood, opened a door and stuck out her head to see how things were going. *Pop!* Up came a troll, whipped off her head, and stuck a calf's head on her shoulders instead. The poor princess ran back into the room on all fours and began to moo like a calf.

When Tatterhood came back and saw her sister, she was very angry that the queen's attendants had not kept better watch. She scolded them all around, and asked what they thought of their carelessness now that her sister had a calf's head.

"I'll see if I can get her free from the troll's spell,"

said Tatterhood. "But I'll need a good ship in full trim and well fitted with stores."

Now the king realized his daughter Tatterhood was quite extraordinary despite her wild ways, so he agreed to this, but said they must have a captain and crew. Tatterhood was firm—she would have no captain or crew. She would sail the ship alone. At last they let her have her way, and Tatterhood sailed off with her sister.

With a good wind behind them, she sailed right to the land of the trolls and tied up at the landing place. She told her sister to stay quite still on board  the ship, but she herself rode her goat right up to the trolls' house. Through an open window she could see her sister's head on the wall. In a trice, she leapt the goat through the window and into the house, snatched the head, and leapt back outside again. She set off with it, and after her came the trolls. They shrieked and swarmed about her like angry bees. But the goat snorted and butted with his horns, and Tatterhood smacked them with her magic wooden spoon until they gave up and let her escape.

When Tatterhood got safely back to their ship, she took off the calf's head and put her sister's own bonny head back on again. Now her sister was once more human.

"Let's sail on and see something of the world," said Tatterhood. Her sister was of the same mind, so they sailed along the coast, stopping at this place and that, until at last they reached a distant kingdom.

Tatterhood tied up the ship at the landing place. When the people of the castle saw the strange sail, they sent down messengers to find out who sailed the ship and whence it came. The messengers were startled to find no one on board but Tatterhood, and she was riding around the deck on her goat.

When they asked if there was anyone else on board, Tatterhood answered that, yes, she had her sister with her. The messengers asked to see her, but Tatterhood said no. They then asked, would the sisters come up to the castle for an audience with the king and his two sons?

"No," said Tatterhood. "Let them come down to the ship if they wish to see us." And she began to gallop about on her goat until the deck thundered.

The elder prince became curious about the strangers and hastened down to the shore the very next day. When he saw the fair younger twin, he promptly fell in love with her and wanted to marry her.

"No indeed," she declared. "I will not leave my sister, Tatterhood. I will not marry until she marries."

The prince went glumly back to the castle, for in his opinion no one would want to marry the odd creature who rode a goat and looked like a ragged beggar. But hospitality must be given to strangers, so the two sisters were invited to a feast at the castle, and the prince begged his younger brother to escort Tatterhood.

The younger twin brushed her hair and put on her finest kirtle* for the event, but Tatterhood refused to change.

"You could wear one of my dresses," said her sister, "instead of that raggedy cloak and old boots." Tatterhood just laughed.

"You might take off that tattered hood and the soot streaks from your face," said her sister crossly, for she wanted her beloved Tatterhood to look her best.

"No," said Tatterhood, "I will go as I am."

All the people of the town turned out to see the strangers riding up to the castle, and a fine proces-

*A kirtle is a skirt.

sion it was! At the head rode the prince and Tatterhood's sister on fine white horses draped with cloth of gold. Next came the prince's brother on a splendid horse with silver trappings. Beside him rode Tatterhood on her goat.

"You're not much for conversation," said Tatterhood. "Haven't you anything to say?"

"What is there to talk about?" he retorted. They rode on in silence until finally he burst out, "Why do you ride on that goat instead of a horse?"

"Since you happened to ask," said Tatterhood, "I can ride on a horse if I choose." At once the goat turned into a fine steed.

Well! The young man's eyes popped open wide, and he turned to look at her with great interest.

"Why do you hide your head beneath that ragged hood?" he asked.

"Is it a ragged hood? I can change it if I choose," she said. And there, on long dark hair, was a circlet of gold and tiny pearls.

"What an unusual girl you are!" he exclaimed. "But that wooden spoon—why do you choose to carry that?"

"Is it a spoon?" And in her hand the spoon turned into a gold-tipped wand of rowan wood.

"I see!" said the prince's brother. He smiled and hummed a little tune as they rode on.

At last Tatterhood said, "Aren't you going to ask me why I wear these ragged clothes?"

"No," said the prince. "It's clear you wear them because you choose to, and when you want to change them, you will."

At that, Tatterhood's ragged cloak disappeared, and she was clad in a velvet green mantle and kirtle. But the prince just smiled and said, "The color becomes you very well."

When the castle loomed up ahead, Tatterhood said to him, "And will you not ask to see my face beneath the streaks of soot?"

"That, too, shall be as you choose."

As they rode through the castle gates, Tatterhood touched the rowan wand to her face, and the soot streaks disappeared. And whether her face now was lovely or plain we shall never know, because it didn't matter in the least to the prince's brother or to Tatterhood.

But this I can tell you: the feast at the castle was a merry one, with the games, and the singing, and the dancing lasting for many days.

PETER C. ASBJØRNSEN *and* JØRGEN MOE *collected this tale in the mid-nineteenth century, and G. W. Dasent translated it for his* Norwegian Folktales *(1859). The magic flowers, the goat, and the wooden spoon may be related to ancient superstitions and symbols. This retelling by the editor is based on Dasent's tale.*

# UNANANA
## and the
## Elephant

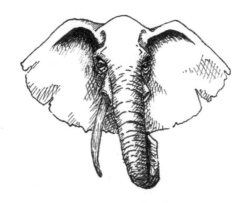

**M**any, many years ago there was a woman called Unanana who had two beautiful children. They lived in a hut near the roadside and people passing by would often stop when they saw the children, exclaiming at the roundness of their limbs, the smoothness of their skin, and the brightness of their eyes.

Early one morning Unanana went into the bush to collect firewood and left her two children playing with a little cousin who was living with them. The children shouted happily, seeing who could jump the farthest, and when they were tired they sat on the dusty ground outside the hut playing a game with pebbles.

Suddenly they heard a rustle in the nearby grasses, and seated on a rock they saw a puzzled-looking baboon.

"Whose children are those?" he asked the little cousin.

"They belong to Unanana," she replied.

"Well, well, well!" exclaimed the baboon in his deep voice. "Never have I seen such beautiful children before."

Then he disappeared and the children went on with their game.

A little later they heard the faint crack of a twig and looking up they saw the big brown eyes of a gazelle staring at them from beside a bush.

"Whose children are those?" she asked the cousin.

"They belong to Unanana," she replied.

"Well, well, well!" exclaimed the gazelle in her soft, smooth voice. "Never have I seen such beautiful children before," and with a graceful bound she disappeared into the bush.

The children grew tired of their game, and taking a small gourd they dipped it in turn into the big pot full of water which stood at the door of their hut, and drank their fill.

A sharp bark made the cousin drop her gourd in fear when she looked up and saw the spotted body and treacherous eyes of a leopard, who had crept silently out of the bush.

"Whose children are those?" he demanded.

"They belong to Unanana," she replied in a

shaky voice, slowly backing toward the door of the hut in case the leopard should spring at her. But he was not interested in a meal just then.

"Never have I seen such beautiful children before," he exclaimed, and with a flick of his tail he melted away into the bush.

The children were afraid of all these animals who kept asking questions and called loudly to Unanana to return, but instead of their mother, a huge elephant with only one tusk lumbered out of the bush and stood staring at the three children, who were too frightened to move.

"Whose children are those?" he bellowed at the little cousin, waving his trunk in the direction of the two beautiful children who were trying to hide behind a large stone.

"They . . . they belong to Una . . . Unanana," faltered the little girl.

The elephant took a step forward.

"Never have I seen such beautiful children before," he boomed. "I will take them away with me," and opening wide his mouth he swallowed both children at a gulp.

The little cousin screamed in terror and dashed into the hut, and from the gloom and safety inside it she heard the elephant's heavy footsteps growing fainter and fainter as he went back into the bush.

It was not until much later that Unanana

returned, carrying a large bundle of wood on her head. The little girl rushed out of the house in a dreadful state and it was some time before Unanana could get the whole story from her.

"Alas! Alas!" said the mother. "Did he swallow them whole? Do you think they might still be alive inside the elephant's stomach?"

"I cannot tell," said the child, and she began to cry even louder than before.

"Well," said Unanana sensibly, "there's only one thing to do. I must go into the bush and ask all the animals whether they have seen an elephant with only one tusk. But first of all I must make preparations."

She took a pot and cooked a lot of beans in it until they were soft and ready to eat. Then seizing her large knife and putting the pot of food on her head, she told her little niece to look after the hut until she returned, and set off into the bush to search for the elephant.

Unanana soon found the tracks of the huge beast and followed them for some distance, but the elephant himself was nowhere to be seen. Presently, as she passed through some tall, shady trees, she met the baboon.

"O baboon! Do help me!" she begged. "Have you seen an elephant with only one tusk? He has eaten both my children and I must find him."

"Go straight along this track until you come to a place where there are high trees and white stones. There you will find the elephant," said the baboon.

So the woman went on along the dusty track for a very long time but she saw no sign of the elephant.

Suddenly she noticed a gazelle leaping across her path.

"O gazelle! Do help me! Have you seen an elephant with only one tusk?" she asked. "He has eaten both my children and I must find him."

"Go straight along this track until you come to a place where there are high trees and white stones. There you will find the elephant," said the gazelle, as she bounded away.

"O dear!" sighed Unanana. "It seems a very long way and I am so tired and hungry."

But she did not eat the food she carried, since that was for her children when she found them.

On and on she went, until rounding a bend in the track she saw a leopard sitting outside his cave-home, washing himself with his tongue.

"O leopard!" she exclaimed in a tired voice. "Do help me! Have you seen an elephant with only one tusk? He has eaten both my children and I must find him."

"Go straight along this track until you come to a place where there are high trees and white stones. There you will find the elephant," replied the leopard, as he bent his head and continued his grooming.

"Alas!" gasped Unanana to herself. "If I do not find this place soon, my legs will carry me no farther."

She staggered on a little farther until suddenly, ahead of her, she saw some high trees with large white stones spread about on the ground below them.

"At last!" she exclaimed, and hurrying forward she found a huge elephant lying contentedly in the shade of the trees. One glance was enough to show her that he had only one tusk, so going up as close as she dared, she shouted angrily:

"Elephant! Elephant! Are you the one that has eaten my children?"

"O no!" he replied lazily. "Go straight along this track until you come to a place where there are huge trees and white stones. There you will find the elephant."

But the woman was sure this was the elephant she sought, and stamping her foot, she screamed at him again:

"Elephant! Elephant! Are you the one that has eaten my children?"

"O no! Go straight along this track—" began the elephant again, but he was cut short by Unanana who rushed up to him waving her knife and yelling:

"Where are my children? Where are they?"

Then the elephant opened his mouth and without even troubling to stand up, he swallowed Unanana with the cooking pot and her knife at one gulp. And this was just what Unanana had hoped for.

Down, down, down she went in the darkness, until she reached the elephant's stomach. What a sight met her eyes! The walls of the elephant's stomach were like a range of hills, and camped among these hills were little groups of people, many dogs and goats and cows, and her own two beautiful children.

"Mother! Mother!" they cried when they saw her. "How did you get here? Oh, we are so hungry."

Unanana took the cooking-pot off her head and began to feed her children with the beans, which they ate ravenously.

The elephant began to groan. His groans could be heard all over the bush, and he said to those animals who came along to find out the cause of his unhappiness:

"I don't know why it is, but ever since I swallowed that woman called Unanana, I have felt most uncomfortable and unsettled inside."

The pain got worse and worse, until with a final grunt the elephant dropped dead. Then Unanana seized her knife and hacked a doorway between the elephant's ribs through which soon streamed a line of dogs, goats, cows, men, women, and children, all blinking their eyes in the strong sunlight and shouting for joy at being free once more.

The animals barked, bleated, or mooed their thanks, while the human beings gave Unanana all kinds of presents in gratitude to her for setting them free, so that when Unanana and her two children reached home, they were no longer poor.

The little cousin was delighted to see them, for she had thought they were all dead, and that night they had a feast. Can you guess what they ate? Yes, roasted elephant meat.

*There is more than one version of this tale to be found among the tribes in the south of Africa. This story is reprinted from* **KATHLEEN ARNOTT**'s African Myths and Legends *(1962).*

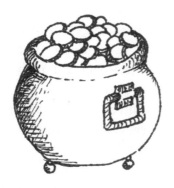

There once was an old woman who earned her living by going on errands and doing odd work for the farmers' wives in the village where she lived. Although she earned only her midday meal and a bit of cheese and bread to bring home for supper, she was always as cheerful as if she hadn't a want in the world. Each day she rose early to gather branches and pine cones. These she laid ready near the hearth, and when she returned home to her cottage in the evening, she made a fire to keep herself warm.

Her cottage was small and poorly furnished. It stood by itself on the outskirts of the village, but she declared she was quite content to live alone, and she didn't mind the long walk home at all.

Nonetheless, the farmers' wives of Hedley made sure to send her on her way before sunset. After dark, the Hedley Kow[*] was abroad, and the Hedley Kow had terrified the villagers since times long past. Whether he was a bogie or a hobgoblin the village folk could not decide, but they did know he could assume fearful shapes and scare people out of their wits. He would chase them home, hooting and bellowing with raucous laughter, and other times he enraged them with all manner of mischief and pranks.

One summer evening as it was getting on toward dark, and the old woman hastened homeward, she came upon a big black pot lying at the side of the road.

"Now *that*," said she, stopping to look at it, "would be just the thing for me if I had anything to put into it! Who can have left it here?" She looked all around to see who it might belong to, but she could see no one either in the fields or on the road.

"Maybe it'll have a hole in it," said she. "Ay, that'll be how they've left it lying. But it'll do fine to put something in. I'm thinking I'll just take it home anyways." And she bent her stiff old back and lifted the lid to look inside.

"Mercy me!" she cried and jumped back. "If it isn't brimful of gold pieces!"

*A kow is a bogie or hobgoblin, and probably pronounced *koo*.

For a while she could do nothing but walk round her treasure, admiring the yellow gold and wondering at her good luck, and saying to herself, "Well, I *do* be feeling rich and grand!" But presently she began to think how she could best take it home with her. She couldn't see any other way than by fastening one end of her shawl to it and so dragging it after her along the road.

"I'll have all the night to think what I'll do with it," she said to herself. "I could buy a grand house and all, and live like a queen; or maybe I'll just bury it in a hole at the foot of the garden; or I could put a bit on the chimney near the teapot, as an ornament. Ah! I feel so grand I don't know myself rightly!"

By this time she was rather tired from dragging such a heavy weight, so she stopped to rest for a minute and turned to make sure her treasure was safe.

But when she looked at it, it wasn't a pot of gold at all, but a great lump of shining silver!

She stared at it, and rubbed her eyes, and stared at it again; but it was still a great lump of silver.

"I'd have sworn it was a pot of gold," she said at last, "but I reckon I must have been dreaming. Ay now, that's a change for the better; it'll be far less trouble to look after and not so easy stolen. Gold pieces are a sight of bother to keep safe. I'm well quit of them, and with my bonny lump of silver I'm as rich as can be!"

She set off homeward again, cheerfully planning all the grand things she was going to do with the money. It wasn't long, however, before she got tired again and stopped once more to rest.

Again she turned to look at her treasure, and as soon as she set eyes on it, she cried out in astonishment. "Oh my! Now it's a lump of iron. Well, that beats all. It's real convenient—I can sell it as easy as easy, and get a lot of pennies for it.

"Ay, it's much handier than a lot of gold and silver that'd keep me awake nights, thinking I'd be robbed. A lump of iron is a good thing to have in the house; you never can tell what you might need it for."

So on she went again, chuckling to herself on her good luck, until presently she glanced over her shoulder just to make sure it was still there.

"Eh, what's this?" she cried as soon as she saw it. "It's gone and turned into a great stone! Now how could it know that I was just wanting something to hold my door open with? Ay, that's a good change. It's a fine thing to have good luck."

And all in a hurry to see how the stone would look in its corner by her door, she trotted off down the hill and stopped at the bottom beside her own gate.

Then she turned around to unfasten her shawl from the stone, which this time seemed to lie quiet and unchanged on the path. She could see the stone quite plainly as she bent her stiff back to untie the shawl end.

All of a sudden, it seemed to give a jump and a squeal, and grew in a moment as big as a great horse. It threw down four lanky legs, shook out two long ears, and flourished a tail. Then it kicked its feet into the air laughing raucously.

The old woman stared as it capered and shrieked and rolled its red shiny eyes.

"Well!" she said at last. "I do be the luckiest body! Fancy me seeing the Hedley Kow all to myself and making so free with it too!"

The Hedley Kow stopped short in its rearing and bellowing to glare at her. "You're not frightened?"

"Not me!" she laughed. "'Tis a rare sight you are!"

"Most folks shout and curse at me," said he, "ay, and run screaming!"

"There's no harm done," she answered cheerfully. "I still have my bit of cheese and bread for my supper."

She gathered her shawl about her and opened her little gate. But when she looked around, instead of the great gangling horse, there stood a small man in a pointed cap scuffling his feet on the path. He was brown as a russet apple, apart from his scraggly white beard.

"Well now," said the old woman kindly, "I don't have much, but you're welcome to come in for a bit of supper."

"Don't mind if I do," said the Hedley Kow.

So he sat down to supper with the old woman, and somehow the bit of cheese became a large chunk, and then there suddenly appeared on the table some nicely boiled brown eggs and crumpets for their tea.

They made a cheerful meal of it, and after they finished they sat beside the fire while the Hedley Kow regaled the old woman with stories of his pranks. She laughed until the tears rolled down her cheeks, and she declared that never had an evening passed so quickly.

As time went on, the little brown man came by often for a bit of supper and an evening of talk. And when the old woman found her woodpile always stacked high and her cupboard always stocked with food, she very wisely said nothing about it to anyone.

The village folk still talked fearfully of the Hedley Kow, or cursed him for his mischief, but the old woman would chuckle and say, "He be not that bad—happens he likes to kick up his heels a bit, he do!"

*The "kow" or hobgoblin haunted the village of Hedley on the Hill in the north of England. It never caused any serious harm, but liked to frighten people and make mischief by changing shapes. This is a retelling by the editor of* **JOSEPH JACOB***'s nine-teenth-century version in* More English Fairy Tales *(1904).*

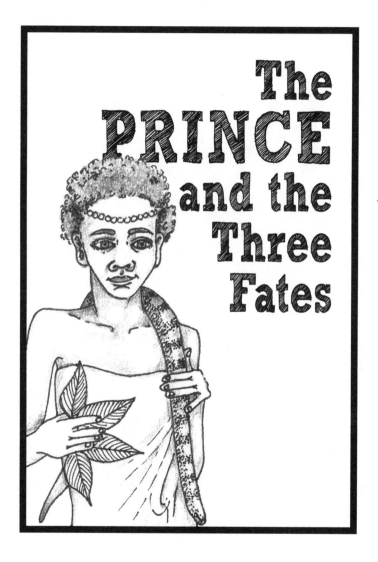

# The
# PRINCE
## and the
## Three
## Fates

Once upon a time a little boy was born to a king and queen who ruled over a country on the banks of the great river Nile. The king and queen joyfully sent messages to all the most powerful peris, or fairy spirits, to come and see this wonderful baby. Within a short time, the fairy spirits were gathered round the cradle.

The king and queen were disturbed to see them look so grave.

"Is there anything the matter?" the king asked anxiously.

The peris all shook their heads at once. "He is a beautiful baby, and it is a great pity, but what is to happen will happen," said they. "It is written in the book of fate that he must die by either a crocodile, a serpent, or a dog. If we could save him we would, but that is beyond our power." And so saying, they vanished.

The king and queen stood horror-stricken at what they had heard. But being of a hopeful nature, they began at once to invent plans to save the prince from the dreadful doom that awaited him. A strong wall was built around their palace, and the child was guarded night and day.

One day, when the boy was six years old, he was sitting at a window when he saw a little dog running and playing outside the walls of the palace. He begged and begged for a dog of his own until the king, feeling sorry for the quiet life his son must lead, said, "Very well, let him have a puppy."

Years went by, and the boy and the dog played together till the boy grew tall and strong. The time came at last when he said to his father, "Why do you keep me shut up here doing nothing? I know all about the prophecy that was made at my birth, but I would far rather be killed at once than live an idle, useless life. Give me arms and let me go, I pray you, and my dog with me."

The king reluctantly granted his plea, knowing his son must now deal with his own fate. The prince and his dog were carried in the palace barge to the other side of the river. A black horse was saddled and waiting for him there, and he mounted and rode away wherever his fancy took him with the dog always at his heels.

Never was a prince so happy, and he rode and

rode until at length he came to a great palace. There he found a number of suitors staying in the guesthouse on the palace grounds, for the princess of this land was being courted by many nobles and princes. She would not accept any of the suitors who thronged the palace, and told them all she was not ready to marry.

The prince was made welcome at the guesthouse with a perfumed bath, as was the custom, and invited to stay for a while. In due course he and the princess became friends, and soon their friendship ripened into love. The princess informed her father that she had made her choice.

At first the king hesitated, saying he knew little about this young man from another country. But the princess was firm; she would marry the prince or no one. So the marriage took place, and great herds of cattle and a large estate were given to the young couple.

A short time afterward, the prince told his wife of the prophecy made at his birth. "My life is in the hands of three creatures," he said. "I am fated to die by a crocodile, a serpent, or a dog."

"How rash you are!" cried the princess, throwing her arms around his neck. "If you know that, how can you have that horrid dog about you? He should be killed at once!"

"Kill my dog who has been my playfellow since

he was a puppy?" he exclaimed. "Never would I allow that!" And all the princess could get from him was a promise that he would always wear a sword and have somebody with him whenever he left the estate.

When the prince and princess had been married a few months, the prince heard that his parents were ill and longing to have their eldest son near them. The young man and his wife set out at once.

They spent the last night of the journey in a town on the banks of the great river. During the night, while the prince was asleep, the princess 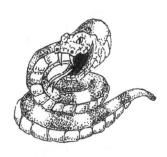 wakened to notice something strange in one corner of the room. It was a dark patch that seemed to grow longer and longer as it moved toward the cushions on which the prince was lying. She shrank in terror making a slight noise, but the creature heard it and raised its head to listen. Then she saw it was the long, flat head of a serpent, and the prophecy rushed into her mind.

Without waking the prince, she glided from her couch and, taking up a heavy bowl of milk which stood on a table, she laid it on the floor in the path of the serpent—for she knew that no serpent can resist milk. She held her breath as the snake drew near. Its eyes fell on the milk. In an instant it was lapping the milk so fast it was a wonder the creature did not choke. When every drop was gone, it dropped on the ground and slept heavily. This was what the princess had been waiting for. Catching up her husband's sword, she severed the snake's head from its body.

The next morning, after this narrow escape, they set out for the king's palace. Here they stayed for a long visit while the prince took over many duties of the kingdom from his father.

One morning, the prince went out with his bow and arrows and his dog to hunt wild duck. While chasing their game, they drew near the reed-covered bank of the river. The prince was running at full speed when he almost fell over something that looked like a log of wood. To his surprise a voice spoke to him, and he saw that what he had taken for a log was really a crocodile.

"You cannot escape from me," it said. "I am your fate, and wherever you go, whatever you do, you will always find me before you. There is only one way of shaking off my power. If you can dig a pit in the dry sand that will remain full of water, my spell will be broken. If not, death will come to you speedily. I give you this one chance. Now go."

The young man walked sadly away, and when he

reached the palace he shut himself into his room. For the rest of the day he refused to see anyone, even his wife. At sunset, however, the princess grew alarmed and demanded to be let in.

"How pale you look," she cried. "Has anything hurt you? Tell me what is the matter for perhaps I can help!" So the prince told her the whole story and of the impossible task given him by the crocodile.

"How can a sand hole remain full of water?" he asked. "Of course it will all run through. The crocodile called it a chance; but he might as well have dragged me into the river at once. He said truly that I cannot escape him."

"Oh, if that is all," cried the princess, "I can set you free myself, for my nurse taught me the use of plants. In the desert, not far from here, there grows a little four-leaved herb which will keep the water in the pit for a whole year. I will go in search of it at dawn, and you can begin to dig the hole as soon as you like."

To comfort her husband the princess had spoken lightly and gaily, but she knew very well she had no light task before her. Still, she was full of courage and energy and determined that her husband should be saved.

It was still starlight when she left the palace on

a snow-white donkey and rode away from the river straight to the west across the desert. For some time she could see nothing before her but a flat waste of sand, which became hotter and hotter as the sun rose. Then a dreadful thirst seized her and the donkey, but there was no stream from which to drink. So she spoke cheering words to her donkey, who brayed in reply, and the two pushed steadily on.

How glad they both were when they caught sight of a tall rock in the distance! They forgot that they were thirsty and the sun hot. The ground seemed to fly under their feet, till the donkey stopped of its own accord in the cool shadow. But though the donkey might rest, the princess could not, for she knew the plant grew on the very top of the rock, and a wide chasm or pit ran round the foot of it.

She had thought to bring a rope with her and, making a noose at one end, she flung it across with all her might. The first time it slid back slowly into the deep pit, and she had to draw it up and throw it, again and again, until at last the noose caught on a jagged point of rock. Now she had to trust her whole weight to the rope, which might snap and let her fall onto the rock below. But nothing so terrible happened. The princess safely reached the other side, and then came the worst part of her task. As fast as she put her foot on a ledge or outcropping of rock to climb, the stone broke away and left her as before. Meanwhile the hours were passing, and it was nearly noon.

She tested several places on the rock face in this way before she found one place more solid than the rest. She managed by great effort to reach it and, finally, with torn and bleeding hands, she gained the top. There was such a violent wind blowing that, almost blinded with sand, she was obliged to throw herself on the ground and feel about for the precious herb.

For a few terrible moments she thought the rock was bare and her journey had been to no purpose. It seemed there was nothing but grit and stones, when suddenly her fingers touched something soft in a crevice. It was a plant, that was clear; but was it the right one? She could not see, for the wind was blowing more fiercely than ever, so she lay where she was and counted the leaves. One, two, three— yes! There were four! And plucking it, she held it safe in her hand while she turned, almost stunned by the wind, to go down the rock.

When once she was safely over the side all became suddenly still, and she slid down the rock so fast that she almost landed in the pit. However, by good luck, she stopped quite close to her rope bridge and was soon across it. The donkey brayed joyfully at the sight of her and set off home across the desert at high speed, never seeming to know that the sand underfoot was nearly as hot as the sun above her.

On the banks of the great rivers she halted, and the princess hurried over to where the prince was standing by the deep hole he had dug in the sand. A huge clay waterpot stood beside him. A little way off, near the bulrushes at the river's edge, the crocodile lay blinking in the sun with his yellow jaws open and his sharp teeth waiting.

At a signal from the princess, the prince poured the water into the hole; and the moment it reached the brim the princess flung in the four-leaved plant.

Would the charm work, or would the water trickle slowly through the sand? For half an hour they stood with their eyes fixed on the spot, but the hole stayed as full as at the beginning, with the little green leaves floating on the top. Then the prince turned with a shout of triumph, and the crocodile sulkily plunged into the river. The prince had escaped forever the second of his three fates!

He stood there looking after the crocodile and

rejoicing that he was free, when he was startled by a wild duck which flew past them, seeking shelter among the reeds and rushes that bordered the river. In another instant his dog dashed by in hot pursuit and knocked heavily against his master's legs.

The prince staggered, lost his balance, and fell backward into the river, where the deep mud and reeds caught him and held him fast. He shouted for help to his wife who came running with the rope she had left coiled near the donkey. The poor old dog was drowned, but the prince was pulled to shore.

"My wife," he said to her gratefully, "has proved stronger than my fate."

*This story is from the Sudanese region of the Nile River. Originally from a collection of ancient Egyptian tales, it was translated and adapted by* **LEONORA BLANCHE ALLEYNE LANG** *for* The Olive Fairy Book *(1907). The present retelling by the editor abridges her story to some extent.*

# JANET
## and
## Tamlin

O nce upon a time in the lowlands of Scotland, there lived an old earl and his bonny daughter, Janet. And on their lands, in the place called Carterhaugh, there stood from ancient times a well belonging to the fairy folk.

Now Janet had the freedom to go wherever she wished except for one place, and that place was the fairy well at Carterhaugh. Indeed, all the village lasses were warned not to tarry at Carterhaugh for it was believed the fairy knights would spirit away any young maid found near the well. Sometimes, village folk who must pass by Carterhaugh left offerings beside the well to please the fairies and bring good luck to themselves.

Janet longed to visit her fairy well to see what she could see. Perhaps she would leave an offering at the well and make a wish for good fortune.

So one fine sunny morning she braided her hair about her head, tucked up her kirtle high above her knees, and hastened off to Carterhaugh as fast as she could go.

The green meadow was filled with the scent of heather and wildflowers, roses and golden broome. Beside the well stood the ancient hawthorn trees, and there Janet hung a silver pin as an offering. She picked a wild rose to tuck in her hair and bent down to peer inside the dark cold water of the well. When she looked up, beside the well grazed a splendid white horse with golden trappings.

Janet moved away uneasily and picked two more roses for her girdle. But, then, standing before her was a young man clad in shimmering green.

"Why do you pick my roses, lady?" he demanded. "Why do you come to Carterhaugh without my leave?"

"Without your leave indeed!" cried Janet. "Carterhaugh is my father's land. I'll come here if I please!"

"The flowers are mine, lady. When you plucked the roses you summoned me."

"I'll pluck a rose if I wish," she answered with spirit. "Who are you to claim the flowers of Carterhaugh?"

"I am the knight Tamlin from the court of the Queen of Elfland."

"I am—Janet," she faltered, and grew afraid for all the warnings and fearful tales she had heard rushed into her mind. Tamlin smiled gently.

"I'll not harm you, Janet."

"Glad I am to hear it, for I've been forbidden to visit the fairy well." She went on ruefully, "It would be a sad thing indeed if they were proved right!"

"Will you tarry awhile, Janet?"

"I will," she said. So they sat and talked together in the fragrant meadow all that summer's day. When evening came Janet returned home, running lightly through the heather.

"No harm has come of it," she said to herself. But she found she thought only of Tamlin, and a few days later she was back at Carterhaugh picking the wild roses at the well. At once Tamlin appeared at her side.

After that Janet went often to the fairy well. Tamlin confessed he haunted the well, waiting for her summons, and Janet thought there was no place she'd rather be than at Carterhaugh with Tamlin.

As the summer waned into autumn, Janet grew sad and quiet. She realized she loved Tamlin, and to love a knight from Elfland was, she knew, a hopeless thing. The maids saw her moping and whispered that Janet had a lover. And her father noticed she was not like her usual merry self at all.

"What ails you, lass?" he asked kindly. "Is it dull here in the castle? Perhaps it's time that you were wed. If there's no young laird you fancy hereabouts, we'll go off to Edinburgh and see what we can find there."

But Janet just shook her head.

The very next day Janet hurried off to Carterhaugh, and when Tamlin stood beside her she said, "Tell me truly, Tamlin, are you a mortal man or fairy spirit?"

"I was a mortal man," he sighed. "I was the Earl of Roxburgh's grandson. But one day riding on the hunt, my horse stumbled and I was thrown hard to the ground. 'Twas on a fairy hill, so as I lay stunned, the Queen of Elfland seized me and took me in to be her knight.

"I liked it very well at first. Now, since I've met you, Janet, I want to return to the real world. If I were free I'd ask your pledge to marry me."

"And I'd say yes," answered Janet. "Is there no way you can leave the fairy world?"

Tamlin shook his head sadly. "The Queen's enchantment is strong, and she has refused to let me go."

"I'll marry no one but you, Tamlin, and I'll not give you up easily. Is there no way to break the enchantment?"

"There's but one way to free me. It's a fearful way, and I doubt that any mortal lass could do it."

"I will do it," said Janet, "if you will tell me what it is."

"Next week comes Halloween. On that night the Queen and all her knights and company ride abroad. You must wait for us near the well at Miles Cross, but stay hidden; you must not be seen. At midnight we will be riding past. It is then you must run out and drag me from my horse."

"How will I know which is you among all that company, Tamlin?"

"Let the first group of three riders pass, and then the second. I will be in the third company. One knight will ride a black steed, the other a brown. But I will ride a pale gray steed on the outer side. My right hand will be gloved, my left hand bare. By this you will know me."

"I will be there," she promised.

"Run quickly to the gray steed and pull the rider down. The fairy host will raise the cry, 'Tamlin is away!' Hold me fast and do not let me go. They'll change me to a wild beast or a snake, but you must hold me fast within your arms, no matter what terrible shape I take. Fear not, I'll do you no harm. They'll turn me into a red-hot bar of iron, and at the very last, they'll turn me into a burning coal. Then quickly throw the coal into the well water, and I'll become a human naked man. Cover me with your cloak and keep me out of sight until the fairy host are gone."

"I will do all that," said Janet. "I will not fail you, Tamlin."

An hour or two before midnight on Halloween, Janet quietly left the sleeping castle. The night was dark and gloomy, and the large branches of the ancient oaks creaked and groaned with the wind. She wrapped her cloak around her and set out for Miles Cross. The dry leaves on the path skittered and rustled as though they were alive. Dark shadows seemed to press around her as she hurried on.

When she reached the well at Miles Cross, she hid herself in the bracken and bushes nearby. Here there was no sound but the wind sighing through the trees. She waited so long she feared the fairy host would not be coming that night.

Then a little before midnight she heard the jingle of fairy bells on bridles. The music of the bells grew clearer, and the strange elfin glow of fairy folk showed her the Queen riding at the head of the fairy company.

Her long golden hair gleamed as it lay over her shoulders and her shimmering green mantle.

A company of three knights rode behind her, and behind them a second company of knights. Janet let them pass. In the third company were a knight on a black steed and a knight on a brown. The third knight, on the pale gray steed, rode on the outer side. His right hand was gloved, his left hand bare.

Janet ran out to the pale gray steed and caught the bridle. She seized hold of the knight and dragged him to the ground. From the fairy host a fearful shriek rang out: "Tamlin is away!"

She felt Tamlin shrink in her arms to become a slippery, wriggling lizard, but she held it fast. The lizard turned into a scaly snake, twisting and coiling in her arms, but she did not let it go.

The snake became a lean wolf with wide snapping jaws, but she gripped it tightly in her arms and did not let it go. The wolf turned into a large shaggy bear with huge paws and sharp teeth. She dug her fingers into the fur and hung on with all her might.

The bear became a fierce lion with large fangs who threw her to the ground, but she held fast and did not let go.

Then the lion became a bar of red-hot iron in her hands. She gritted her teeth and staggered to her feet, but would not drop it. At last the iron bar became a glowing coal, and this she threw into the well.

A cry of rage went up from the fairy host. By the unearthly elfin light she saw Tamlin climb naked from the well and quickly threw her cloak over him, hiding him from their sight.

The Queen cried out angrily to Janet, "You have taken my best knight! If I had known Tamlin would be taken from me, I'd have turned his eyes to wood and his heart to stone!"

With that, the fairy host rode off into the night, the eerie glow fading, the golden bridle bells jingling faintly in the distance.

In the silence and the dark, Janet crouched near the well still holding Tamlin closely in her arms. She knew that Tamlin was now free, and that he would be her heart's delight.

*Several old ballads about Janet and Tamlin from the Border Country of Scotland were used by the editor as a source for this story. Tales of humans captured by the fairies or the Queen of Elfland are frequent in Celtic folklore, but not all end as happily as this one does.*

The Western Mono tribe lived high up on the Kings River. They knew how to use magic. Here is a story they told:

Once there were six pretty Mono wives. These wives had six husbands who were mountain-lion hunters.

One day, while the husbands were out hunting, the wives went up the mountain to pick clover for food. That day, one wife discovered something new to eat—wild onions.

"Yum, these new plants taste better than anything I've ever eaten!" she told the others. "Just taste this."

The other wives all tasted the onions. They liked them too. They ate and ate and smacked their lips and then went home to cook supper for their husbands.

Just as dusk was falling the husbands came plodding home. Each had killed a big mountain lion.

"Phew! What's that odor?" the husbands asked their wives when they got to the hut door.

They came closer to their wives and discovered the terrible odor was on the breath of their wives!

"We found this new plant to eat—just taste it," the wives said and offered some to the husbands.

"No!" they cried in disgust. "Your breath enough for us—horrible!" They wouldn't even taste the onions.

That night the husbands made their wives stay outdoors because the odor of onions kept them awake.

It was cold outside and the wives didn't like to stay out there alone without their husbands.

The next day when the husbands had gone hunting, the wives went back to where the onions grew and ate more than they had the day before. Those onions were so tasty, they just couldn't help eating them.

When the husbands came home for supper, not one of them had slain a mountain lion. Never before had they come home without mountain lions and they were very sad.

"Mountain lions smelled that horrible odor on

us," they grumbled. "Mountain lions ran away fast before we could get near enough to catch them."

The wives didn't believe their husbands and said so.

But when the husbands smelled the odor of onions stronger than ever, they scolded, "You can't come near us! You are worse than skunks."

Again, they wouldn't let their wives come inside the hut to sleep. They wouldn't put food out for their wives to eat.

The wives went home to their fathers and mothers, but that didn't do any good. They were sent right back to their husbands.

This lasted six days. Each night the men came home without mountains lions and each night they found their wives had been eating onions again.

Finally, what with the strong odor of onions and not getting mountain lions, the husbands went into a terrible rage.

"Go away!" they shouted. "Go away! We can't hunt! We can't sleep nights because you eat so many onions. We don't want you anymore. Go away!"

The next morning when the husbands had gone, the wives all went up the mountain to where onions grew. Each of them took her magic rope made of eagle's down.

They were hungry and missed the mush, and they were tired of sleeping alone in the cold outside the hut at night.

"Let's leave our husbands forever," one wife said. "Our husbands don't like us anymore."

They all agreed.

So they climbed and climbed up a big rock. Each wife carried her eagle-down rope. One wife brought her little girl with her.

At last, they reached the very top of the rock. They rested awhile, then the leader of the wives said, "Now is the time for magic. Do you still want to leave your husbands forever?"

"Yes!" they all cried.

So the leader of the wives said a magic Mono word and threw her eagle-down rope up into the sky.

*Whoosh!* it went, straight up. The center of the rope caught on a piece of the sky so that both ends of the rope hung down to the rock.

The women tied all their own ropes to the ends of the rope hanging from the sky. Then they clasped hands and called:

"Eagle-down ropes, magic ropes, help us!"

They stood on the ropes which were spread on the rock and began to sing to the magic ropes, with a special magic song, the ropes slowly began to rise and swing around and around the way Buzzard flies.

As the wives sang louder the ropes made bigger and bigger circles in the sky.

Soon the women standing on the ropes were sailing through the sky over the village where they lived.

Their fathers and mothers looked up and saw them in the sky. People of the village pointed up at them and were very excited.

The women in the sky saw their mothers and fathers and their mothers-in-law and fathers-in-law rush into huts. Next they saw them come out with mush and beads and belts and put all these things on the ground.

"Come back!" the women's relatives cried up at them. "Come back and see what we have for you!"

But the women just stayed in the sky.

Down below, the husbands looked up and saw their wives. "Why didn't you keep an eye on them?" they scolded their wives' parents. "Why did you let them get away when we were out hunting?"

Now that the wives were gone, the husbands wanted them back. They were lonesome and sad. They got together and tried to think what to do.

They decided to use their own magic eagle-down ropes and go up in the sky after their wives.

They climbed the rock, put down their ropes

and sang in the same way their wives had done. Soon they were sailing in the sky over the village.

Old people came out and begged their sons to come back, but the sons wanted their wives, so they kept on singing and going higher and higher into the sky.

By this time the wives were very high in the sky because they had a head start on the husbands. They looked down and saw their husbands coming after them.

"Shall we let them catch us?" they asked each other.

"No!" said one. "Our husbands said they didn't want us anymore. Don't let them catch up with us, ever."

All agreed they would rather be alone in the sky.

As soon as the husbands got close enough, the women shouted down. "Stay where you are!"

The wives had stronger magic in their eagle-down ropes and their song. The men had to stay right where they were—below their wives.

They all turned into stars where they are to this day.

White people call the higher group of six stars the Pleiades. Native Americans call them the Young Women. The lower set of six stars, white people call Taurus. Native Americans call them the Young Men.

Whatever the name, there they are, swinging slowly across the sky on clear nights—and all because the Mono women loved to eat wild onions more than any-thing else.

**ANNE FISHER** *retells this tale in* Stories California Indians Told *(1957). Many Native American tales are mythic stories which explain the natural world. Native Americans in different parts of the country have different stories to explain how the constellations appeared.*

# KATE
## CRACKERNUTS

Once upon a time, far to the north of Scotland, there lived a king and a queen. The king had a daughter, Anne, and the noblewoman he married had a daughter named Kate. The two girls grew to love each other dearly.

However, after a time the new queen became jealous of Anne, thinking her bonnier than her own daughter, Kate. It was a foolish notion, for the two girls were both fine lasses, one fair-haired, one dark-haired. Nonetheless the foolish queen said to herself, "Should a prince come riding by, Anne will surely marry him; and her father would settle the kingdom on the pair, no doubt!"

This fretted her mind sorely till at last she went to consult a local henwife who was known for her magic potions and spells. The henwife took the queen's gold piece and told her she knew a magic spell that would suit her purpose. "Send the lassie to me early in the morn," she said, "but be sure 'tis before she's had food or drink."

So early the next morning the queen said to Anne, "Go, my dear, to the henwife in the glen and ask her for fresh eggs." Anne set out, but as she passed through the kitchen, she saw a crust of bread. Being quite hungry, she took it and munched it as she went along.

When she reached the cottage, Anne said, "The queen has sent me for fresh eggs."

"Come in, lass," said the henwife. "Now lift the lid off that pot and see what you'll see!" Anne did this, but nothing happened.

The henwife said crossly, "Go home to the queen and tell her to keep her larder door better locked!"

Anne took the eggs and went home to the queen to tell her what the henwife had said. The queen knew from this that Anne had had something to eat, so she watched carefully the next morning and sent Anne away fasting. But the princess saw some country folk picking peas by the roadside, and being a friendly lass, she stopped to talk with them. They offered her a handful of fresh peas, and these she took to eat on the way.

When she told the henwife she had come for eggs, the henwife said, "Lift the lid off that pot and see what you'll see!" Anne lifted the lid and peered in, but still nothing happened. Then the henwife was rare angry and said, "Tell the queen the pot won't boil if the fire's away." Anne went home and told this to the queen.

The third day the queen went along with Anne to the henwife to make sure Anne had neither food nor drink. Now this time, when Anne lifted the lid off the pot to peer inside, her bonny head was suddenly turned into a sheep's head. The queen was dismayed. She had not intended anything so drastic to happen to Anne.

How the maids in the castle stared and tittered when they saw Anne! As for Kate, she said she would bide at home no longer. She would go out into the world to seek her fortune and take her sister Anne with her. So she wrapped a fine linen kerchief about her sister's face and head and off they went with a bannock* to eat on the way.

They walked on and on, over a mountain and down the other side, till at last they came to a castle. Kate knocked at the door and asked a night's lodging for herself and her sick sister.

The two sisters were fed and given a room, but they were not long in the castle before Kate saw something was amiss.

*A bannock is a round bread made of oatmeal or barley.

Such lamenting and grieving among the castle folk! She learned the young prince had a strange illness and no one could discover what ailed him. He lay abed, pale and weak, sleeping so heavily all the day that no one could rouse him. The king was fair beside himself with worry, and he had offered a peck of gold to anyone who could restore the prince to health. But the curious thing, the castle folk told Kate, was that anyone who sat up all night with the prince was never seen again.

"A peck of gold is a fine fortune," Kate said to Anne. "With that we could seek out a way to break the wicked spell on you." So Kate went to the king and said she would try to discover what ailed the prince.

The king shook his head in doubt. "It's a strange matter surely. All manner of herb remedies and word charms have been tried, and doctors brought in." Reluctantly, he gave orders for Kate to be brought to the prince's chamber.

When Kate saw the pale young prince sleeping so heavily, she felt a great pity for him. She was a brave girl, and she was determined she would sit up with him through the night to see what she could see.

That night the prince slept on, and Kate sat in a chair before the fire. All was quiet in the castle until midnight. Then suddenly up rose the sick prince from his bed, dressed himself, and went down the stairs. His eyes were open, but he did not notice Kate. He seemed like one asleep or entranced. Kate followed him quietly.

The prince went to the stable where he saddled and mounted his horse. Kate leapt lightly up behind him. Away rode the prince and Kate through the greenwood. The moon shone faintly through the trees, and Kate saw the branches on either side of them were heavy with hazelnuts. She plucked the nuts as they passed, filling both her pockets with them.

They rode on and on until at last they came to a green hill, a high, grass-covered mound. Here the prince drew rein and called, "Open! Open green hill and let the young prince in."

"And the lady behind him," added Kate.

The green hill opened, and the prince dismounted. Kate quickly slid off the horse and hid in the shadows near the entrance. The prince entered a magnificent great hall brilliantly lit as though by thousands of candles. But candles there were none—it was the light given off by all the fairy host gathered there. Fair, shimmering fairy women surrounded the prince and led him off to the dance. The prince danced on and on to the fairy music till he could dance no longer and fell upon a couch. Then the fairy women would fan him for a few minutes and bring him right back into the dance.

At last the cock crowed, and Kate slipped outside the fairy hill. The prince made haste to leave the great hall. The hill closed behind them, and the prince climbed wearily onto his horse. Kate mounted behind him, and home they rode.

When the castle servants came into the prince's chamber in the morning, they found the prince heavily asleep in his bed and Kate beside the fire cracking the nuts she had gathered. But naught did she say of what had happened in the night until she went back to her sister's chamber. Then Kate told her sister of the fairy hill. She had found the cause of the prince's strange sickness, but she knew no way to break the fairies' spell.

Anne became very alarmed, and begged Kate not to follow the prince through the greenwood again. "If the fairies discover you there, they will be angry—they will keep you under that fairy hill for seven years!" But Kate said she must go if the prince again rode off at night.

The second night passed in the same way. The prince rose at midnight and rode off to the fairy hill, Kate astride behind him. Again she gathered nuts from the trees and filled her pockets. This time after the prince had entered the great hall, Kate crept a little closer to watch and listen. She could hear the fairy women speak to each other, and she saw a small fairy child playing nearby. Again the prince whirled and leapt and danced to the fairy music.

"The bonny prince will not last much longer in the outer world," said one fairy woman as she  danced past. "Then he will be with us forever!" Kate felt despair when she heard this. She turned away from the merry dancers to watch the fairy child, hardly more than a babe, playing with a small polished stick the shape of a shepherd's crook. She heard one fairy woman say, "The babe should not be playing with the rowan wand." But the other shrugged and answered, "No matter. 'Tis only a charm against sheep's head spells." The fairies danced on.

Kate knew she must have that rowan crook, so she rolled some of the nuts from her pocket till the babe dropped the stick and went after the nuts. Kate quickly reached out for the crook and put it into her pocket.

At cockcrow they rode home as before. Kate hurried to her sister's room and touched Anne's head three times with the rowan crook. The dreadful sheep's head disappeared, and Anne was once more her own bonny self!

But the prince still lay abed, heavily asleep, paler and thinner than ever. Kate said she would sit up with the prince one more night.

At midnight on the third night the prince rose as before. Kate followed him, leapt onto the horse behind him, and together they rode through the greenwood. Once more she plucked the nuts from the branches as they passed and filled her pockets.

Once more the prince danced and whirled in the fairy hill, while Kate, hidden close by the entrance, watched and listened to all that was said. This night

a fairy child was playing nearby with a small willow basket, and Kate heard one woman say, "'Tis not wise to let the child have that with the prince here."

But the other laughed and said, "The prince doesn't know that to eat of that bird would break our spell!"

Kate rolled out her nuts, one after another, until the basket was dropped, and the child followed the nuts. Kate quickly reached out for the little basket and put it into her pocket.

At cockcrow they returned home to the castle. The prince undressed and fell into bed. Kate undid the latch and opened the basket. She took out the strange bird, plucked the feathers, and cooked the bird over the fire. Soon a savory smell filled the room.

The prince awoke and cried out, "Oh, I wish I had a bite of that bird!"

So Kate gave him a bite, and he rose up on one elbow. Kate gave him a second bite, and he sat up on his bed. Then he said, "If I had but a third bite of that bird . . . !" So Kate gave him a third bite, and he stood up hale and strong.

He dressed himself and sat down by the hearth. When the castle folk came in the next morning, they found Kate and the young prince cracking nuts together and roasting them over the fire.

Great was the feasting and celebration of the young prince's recovery! And you may be sure that Kate and Anne, as honored guests, joined in dancing and games right merrily. The folk in the Orkney Islands still tell of it, for the feasting and the drinking and the merrymaking went on for seven weeks. And they say that all who were there "lived happy, died happy, and never drank out of a dry cappy.*"

*A cappy is a cup.

*The original and only version of this tale was collected in the nine-teenth century from an elderly woman in the Orkney Islands off the north coast of Scotland.*

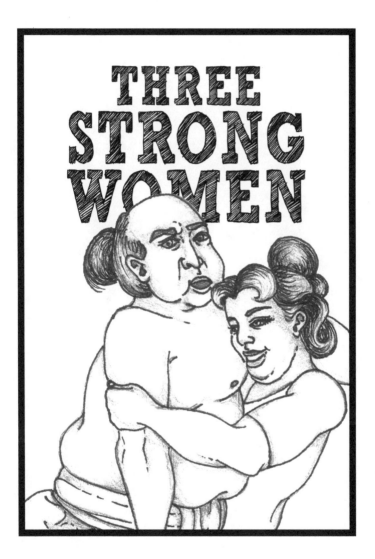

L ong ago, in Japan, there lived a famous wrestler, and he was on his way to the capital city to wrestle before the Emperor.

He strode down the road on legs thick as the trunks of small trees. He had been walking for seven hours and could, and probably would, walk for seven more without getting tired.

The time was autumn, the sky was a cold, watery blue, the air chilly. In the small bright sun, the trees along the roadside glowed red and orange.

The wrestler hummed to himself, "Zun-zun-zun," in time with the long swing of his legs. Wind blew through his thin brown robe, and he wore no sword at his side. He felt proud that he needed no sword, even in the darkest and loneliest places. The icy air on his body only reminded him that few tailors would have been able to make expensive warm clothes for a man so broad and tall. He felt much as a wrestler should—strong, healthy, and rather conceited.

A soft roar of fast-moving water beyond the trees told him that he was passing above a river bank. He "zun-zunned" louder; he loved the sound of his voice and wanted it to sound clearly above the rushing water.

He thought: They call me Forever-Mountain because I am such a good strong wrestler—big, too. I'm a fine, brave man and far too modest ever to say so . . .

Just then he saw a girl who must have come up from the river, for she steadied a bucket on her head.

Her hands on the bucket were small, and there was a dimple on each thumb, just below the knuckle. She was a round girl with red cheeks and a nose like a friendly button. Her eyes looked as though she were thinking of ten thousand funny stories at once. She clambered up onto the road and walked ahead of the wrestler, jolly and bounceful.

"If I don't tickle that fat girl, I shall regret it all my life," said the wrestler under his breath. "She's sure to go 'squeak' and I shall laugh and laugh. If she drops her bucket, that will be even funnier—and I can always run and fill it again and even carry it home for her."

He tiptoed up and poked her lightly in the ribs with one huge finger.

"Kochokochokocho!" he said, a fine, ticklish sound in Japanese.

The girl gave a satisfying squeal, giggled, and brought one arm down so that the wrestler's hand was caught between it and her body.

"Ho-ho-ho! You've caught me! I can't move at all!" said the wrestler, laughing.

"I know," said the jolly girl.

He felt that it was very good-tempered of her to take a joke so well, and started to pull his hand free.

Somehow, he could not.

He tried again, using a little more strength.

"Now, now—let me go," he said. "I am a very powerful man. If I pull too hard I might hurt you."

"Pull," said the girl. "I admire powerful men."

She began to walk, and though the wrestler tugged and pulled until his feet dug great furrows in the ground, he had to follow. She couldn't have paid him less attention if he had been a puppy—a small one.

Ten minutes later, still tugging while trudging helplessly after her, he was glad that the road was lonely and no one was there to see.

"Please let me go," he pleaded. "I am the famous wrestler Forever-Mountain. I must go and show my strength before the Emperor"—he burst out weeping from shame and confusion—"and you're hurting my hand!"

The girl steadied the bucket on her head with her free hand and smiled sympathetically over her shoulder. "You poor, sweet little Forever-Mountain," she said. "Are you tired? Shall I carry you? I can leave the water here and come back for it later."

"I do not want you to carry me. I want you to let me go, and then I want to forget I ever saw you. What do you want with me?" moaned the pitiful wrestler.

"I only want to help you," said the girl, now pulling him steadily up and up a narrow mountain path. "Oh, I am sure you'll have no more trouble than anyone else when you come up against the other wrestlers. You'll win, or else you'll lose, and you won't be too badly hurt either way. But aren't you afraid you might meet a really strong man someday?"

Forever-Mountain turned white. He stumbled. He was imagining being laughed at throughout Japan as "Hardly-Ever-Mountain."

She glanced back.

"You see? Tired already," she said. "I'll walk more slowly. Why don't you come along to my mother's house and let us make a strong man of you? The wrestling in the capital isn't due to begin for three months. I know, because Grandmother thought she'd go. You'd be spending all that time in bad company and wasting what little power you have."

"All right. Three months. I'll come along," said the wrestler. He felt he had nothing more to lose. Also, he feared that the girl might become angry if he refused, and place him in the top of a tree until he changed his mind.

"Fine," she said happily. "We are almost there."

She freed his hand. It had become red and a little swollen. "But if you break your promise and run off, I shall have to chase you and carry you back."

Soon they arrived in a small valley. A simple farmhouse with a thatched roof stood in the middle.

"Grandmother is at home, but she is an old lady and she's probably sleeping." The girl shaded her eyes with one hand. "But Mother should be bringing our cow back from the field—oh, there's Mother now!"

She waved. The woman coming around the corner of the house put down the cow she was carrying and waved back.

She smiled and came across the grass, walking with a lively bounce like her daughter. Well, maybe her bounce was a little more solid, thought the wrestler.

"Excuse me," she said, brushing some cow hair from her dress and smiling, also like her daughter. "These mountain paths are full of stones. They hurt the cow's feet. And who is the nice young man you've brought, Maru-me?"

The girl explained. "And we have only three months!" she finished anxiously.

"Well, it's not long enough to do much, but it's not so short a time we can't do something," said her mother, looking thoughtful. "But he does look terribly feeble. He'll need a lot of good things to eat. Maybe when he gets stronger he can help Grandmother with some of the easy work about the house."

"That will be fine!" said the girl, and she called her grandmother—loudly, for the old lady was a little deaf.

"I'm coming!" came a creaky voice from inside the house, and a little old woman leaning on a stick and looking very sleepy tottered out of the door. As she came toward them she stumbled over the roots of a great oak tree.

"Heh! My eyes aren't what they used to be. That's the fourth time this month I've stumbled over that tree," she complained and, wrapping her skinny arms about its trunk, pulled it out of the ground.

"Oh, Grandmother! You should have let me pull it up for you," said Maru-me.

"Hm. I hope I didn't hurt my poor old back," muttered the old lady. She called out, "Daughter! Throw that tree away like a good girl, so no one will fall over it. But make sure it doesn't hit anybody."

"You can help Mother with the tree," Maru-me said to Forever-Mountain. "On second thought, you'd better not help. Just watch."

Her mother went to the tree, picked it up in her two hands, and threw it. Up went the tree, sailing end over end, growing smaller and smaller as it flew. It landed with a faint crash far up the mountainside.

"Ah, how clumsy," she said. "I meant to throw it over the mountain. It's probably blocking the path now, and I'll have to get up early tomorrow to move it."

The wrestler was not listening. He had very quietly fainted.

"Oh! We must put him to bed," said Maru-me.

"Poor, feeble young man," said her mother.

"I hope we can do something for him. Here, let me carry him, he's light," said the grandmother. She slung him over her shoulder and carried him into the house, creaking along with her cane.

The next day they began the work of making Forever-Mountain over into what they thought a strong man should be. They gave him the simplest food to eat, and the toughest. Day by day they prepared his rice with less and less water, until no ordinary man could have chewed or digested it.

Every day he was made to do the work of five men, and every evening he wrestled with Grandmother. Maru-me and her mother agreed that Grandmother, being old and feeble, was the least likely to injure him accidentally. They hoped the exercise might be good for the old lady's rheumatism.

He grew stronger and stronger but was hardly aware of it. Grandmother could still throw him easily into the air—and catch him again—without ever changing her sweet old smile.

He quite forgot that outside this valley he was one of the greatest wrestlers in Japan and was called Forever-Mountain. His legs had been like logs; now they were like pillars. His big hands were hard as stones, and when he cracked his knuckles the sound was like trees splitting on a cold night.

Sometimes he did an exercise that wrestlers do in Japan—raising one foot high above the ground and bringing it down with a crash. Then people in nearby villages looked up at the winter sky and told one another that it was very late in the year for thunder.

Soon he could pull up a tree as well as the grandmother. He could even throw one—but only a small distance. One evening, near the end of his third month, he wrestled with Grandmother and held her down for half a minute.

"Heh-heh!" she chortled and got up, smiling with every wrinkle. "I would never have believed it!"

Maru-me squealed with joy and threw her arms around him—gently, for she was afraid of cracking his ribs.

"Very good, very good! What a strong man," said her mother, who had just come home from the fields, carrying, as usual, the cow. She put the cow down and patted the wrestler on the back.

They agreed that he was now ready to show some *real* strength before the Emperor.

"Take the cow along with you tomorrow when you go," said the mother. "Sell her and buy yourself a belt—a silken belt. Buy the fattest and heaviest one you can find. Wear it when you appear before the Emperor, as a souvenir from us."

"I wouldn't think of taking your only cow. You've already done too much for me. And you'll need her to plow the fields, won't you?"

They burst out laughing. Maru-me squealed; her mother roared. The grandmother cackled so hard and long that she choked and had to be pounded on the back.

"Oh dear," said the mother, still laughing. "You didn't think we used our cow for anything like *work*! Why, Grandmother here is stronger than five cows!"

"The cow is our pet." Maru-me giggled. "She has lovely brown eyes."

"But it really gets tiresome having to carry her back and forth each day so that she has enough grass to eat," said her mother.

"Then you must let me give you all the prize money that I win," said Forever-Mountain.

"Oh, no! We wouldn't think of it!" said Maru-me. "Because we all like you too much to sell you anything. And it is not proper to accept gifts of money from strangers."

"True," said Forever-Mountain. "I will now ask your mother's and grandmother's permission to marry you. I want to be one of the family."

"Oh! I'll get a wedding dress ready!" said Maru-me.

The mother and grandmother pretended to consider very seriously, but they quickly agreed.

Next morning Forever-Mountain tied his hair

up in the topknot that all Japanese wrestlers wear, and got ready to leave. He thanked Maru-me and her mother and bowed very low to the grand-mother, since she was the oldest and had been a fine wrestling partner.

Then he picked up the cow in his arms and trudged up the mountain. When he reached the top, he slung the cow over one shoulder and waved goodbye to Maru-me.

At the first town he came to, Forever-Mountain sold the cow. She brought a good price because she was unusually fat from never having worked in her life. With the money, he bought the heaviest silken belt he could find.

When he reached the palace grounds, many of the other wrestlers were already there, sitting about, eating enormous bowls of rice, comparing one another's weight, and telling stories. They paid little attention to Forever-Mountain except to wonder why he had arrived so late this year. Some of them noticed that he had grown very quiet and took no part at all in their boasting.

All the ladies and gentlemen of the court were waiting in a special courtyard for the wrestling to begin. They wore many robes, one on top of another, heavy with embroidery and gold cloth, and sweat ran down their faces and froze in the winter afternoon. The gentlemen had long swords so weighted with gold and precious stones that they could never have used them, even if they had known how. The court ladies, with their long black hair hanging down behind, had their faces painted dead white, which made them look frightened. They had pulled out their real eyebrows and painted new ones high above the place where eyebrows are supposed to be, and this made them all look as though they were very surprised at something.

Behind a screen sat the Emperor—by himself, because he was too noble for ordinary people to look at. He was a lonely old man with a kind, tired face. He hoped the wrestling would end quickly so that he could go to his room and write poems.

The first two wrestlers chosen to fight were Forever-Mountain and a wrestler who was said to have the biggest stomach in the country. He and Forever-Mountain both threw some salt into the ring. It was understood that this drove away evil spirits.

Then the other wrestler, moving his stomach somewhat out of the way, raised his foot and brought it down with a fearful stamp. He glared fiercely at Forever-Mountain as if to say, "Now you stamp, you poor frightened man!"

Forever-Mountain raised his foot. He brought it down.

There was a sound like thunder, the earth shook, and the other wrestler bounced into the air and out of the ring, as gracefully as any soap bubble.

He picked himself up and bowed to the Emperor's screen.

"The earth-god is angry. Possibly there is something the matter with the salt," he said. "I do not think I shall wrestle this season." And he walked out, looking very suspiciously over one shoulder at Forever-Mountain.

Five other wrestlers then and there decided that they were not wrestling this season, either. They all looked annoyed with Forever-Mountain.

From then on, Forever-Mountain brought his foot down lightly. As each wrestler came into the ring, he picked him up very gently, carried him out, and placed him before the Emperor's screen, bowing most courteously every time.

The court ladies' eyebrows went up even higher. The gentlemen looked disturbed and a little afraid. They loved to see fierce, strong men tugging and grunting at each other, but Forever-Mountain was a little too much for them. Only the Emperor was happy behind his screen, for now, with the wrestling over so quickly, he would have that much more time to write his poems. He ordered all the prize money handed over to Forever-Mountain.

"But," he said, "you had better not wrestle anymore." He stuck a finger through his screen and waggled it at the other wrestlers, who were sitting on the ground weeping with disappointment like great fat babies.

Forever-Mountain promised not to wrestle anymore. Everybody looked relieved. The wrestlers sitting on the ground almost smiled.

"I think I shall become a farmer," Forever-Mountain said, and left at once to go back to Maru-me.

Maru-me was waiting for him. When she saw him coming, she ran down the mountain, picked him up, together with the heavy bags of prize money, and carried him halfway up the mountainside. Then she giggled and put him down. The rest of the way she let him carry her.

Forever-Mountain kept his promise to the Emperor and never fought in public again. His name was forgotten in the capital. But up in the mountains, sometimes, the earth shakes and rumbles, and they say that is Forever-Mountain and Maru-me's grandmother practicing wrestling in the hidden valley.

*According to the author* **CLAUS STAMM**, *this folktale is still told in Japan. Stamm's version of the tall story reprinted here originally appeared in 1962.*

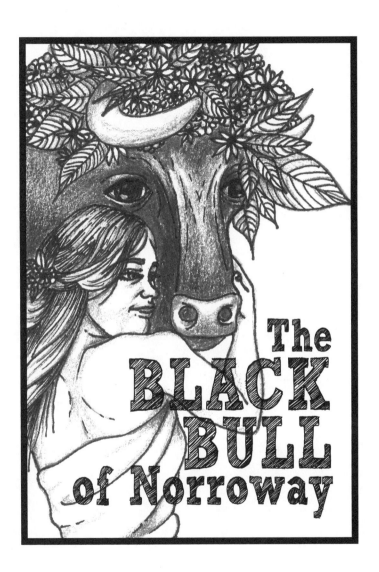

The
BLACK
BULL
of Norroway

L ong ago in Norroway there lived a woman who had three daughters. Off they went one day to learn their fortunes from an old woman who lived in the forest. The oldest daughter was told she would marry an earl, the second daughter that she would marry a lord, and the youngest—a black bull.

The two older sisters were very pleased with their fortunes, but the youngest sister laughed and said, "No matter, I'll be content with the Black Bull of Norroway!"

Her sisters warned her not to jest of such a monster, lest it become true.

"I'm not so eager to marry," she declared. "I'll stay at home until the Black Bull comes to court me."

Well, the two older sisters went out into the

world, and one did marry an earl, and the other did marry a lord. Nonetheless, the youngest sister was quite surprised one day to see a great big black bull at the door. At first the girl was afraid, but the bull seemed gentle and quiet. He looked at her with steady eyes and said he'd come to fetch her.

"I promised I would be content with the Black Bull of Norroway," she said to her mother, "and I will keep my word." So she climbed onto his back and off they went. And always the Bull chose the smoothest paths, the easiest roads, and was careful not to brush against thorns and briers.

On they rode until the girl was almost faint with hunger. The Black Bull said to her in a soft, friendly voice, "Reach into my right ear, and you will find food. Reach into my left ear, and you will find drink." She did so, and after drinking and eating, she gathered the remains in her kerchief to eat later.

Toward evening they came in sight of a fine castle. "Yonder lives my eldest brother," said the Black Bull, "and there we must stay tonight."

When they arrived at the castle the girl was made welcome, and the Black Bull was sent out to the fields with others of his kind. The next morning before she took her leave, she was given a golden walnut by the people in the castle. They told her not to break it open until she was in the worst trouble ever a person could be, and then it would help her.

She climbed onto the back of the Black Bull, and they traveled on through forests and over mountains. From the Black Bull's right ear she had food, and from his left ear she had drink. On the way they talked with each other, and the girl found him a cheerful companion.

When evening drew near, they came in sight of a castle grander than the first one. The Black Bull said, "Yonder my second brother lives, and there we must stay this night." The girl was made welcome by the people of the castle, and this time she asked that the Black Bull be fed well and stabled, for she had become very fond of him.

The next morning, before they set off again, she was given a large golden hickory nut by the castle folk. They told her not to use it until she was in the worst trouble in the world, and it would bring her through it. Again the Black Bull magically provided food and drink, and they talked as they traveled on. That evening they reached a very grand castle. "Yonder lives my youngest brother," said the Bull, "and here we must stay the night."

The girl was made welcome at the castle. But she would not leave the Black Bull until she made sure he was brushed and fed, and settled comfortably in the stable. The next morning she was given a large golden hazelnut by the castle folk. Again she was told not to open it until she was in the worst straits ever, and then it would help her.

Now they rode on and on until they reached a dark and ugsome glen. The Black Bull told her that the time had come for him to try to break his enchantment. The Bull halted, and she slid down from his back.

"Here you must stay while I go on and fight the Old One," said the Bull. "He is powerful, and I do not know what monstrous shape he will be. If I destroy him, the trolls' enchantment will be broken, and I will be once more a man."

The Black Bull then led her to a great rock. "There is one thing you must do. You must sit on this rock and move neither hand nor foot while I'm gone—or I shall never find you again. And if everything round about you turns blue, it means I have beaten the creature; but if all things turn red, he will have conquered me." And with a loud bellow, the Black Bull set out to find his foe.

The girl sat upon the rock, still as could be, moving neither hand nor foot. She waited and waited and waited; then all around her turned blue. In the far distance, through the eerie blue light, she glimpsed the tall and bloodstained figure of a knight. Overcome with joy at her friend's victory, she moved her foot.

Long she waited, but he did not return for the enchantment was but partly broken. And though he searched for her in the glen, he could not find her.

Then she wept, for she knew that by moving her foot, she had failed to help him break the enchantment; he was still under the power of the trolls. She touched the three golden nuts in her pocket, but the time had not yet come to use them. She would search for him and free him if she could.

Wearily she got up and walked on and on for many days, till she came to a great hill of glass. Round the bottom of the hill she went, trying to climb it; but she could not.

At last she came to a smith's forge. The smith promised he would make her iron shoes to climb the hill of glass, if she would work for him for seven months and seven days. She worked in the forge the seven months and seven days, and the smith gave her the iron shoes. He warned her the glass hill led to the country of the trolls, but she paid him no mind and climbed the hill.

When she reached the land of the trolls, she heard talk of a gallant knight who was forced to dwell among them. They were determined the knight should marry one of the troll women, but he had refused even the troll princess. He had said he could marry no one until the blood was washed from his clothes.

It was proclaimed that whoever could wash the knight's garments clean should be his bride. There was a great clatter as one troll woman after another tried to wash the torn, bloodstained garments. Their hairy bodies glistened and their red eyes gleamed as they scrubbed and washed, but the blood stains would not come out.

When the troll princess saw the strange girl who had come into their land, she set her to work washing the knight's bloody garments. When the girl washed the clothes, the stains came out at once, leaving the garments pure and clean. But the troll princess brought the garments to the captive knight and claimed that she herself had washed them clean, and that she would marry him.

Now the girl was in despair. The marriage was to be held the next day. How could she save him? Surely this was the time to open the golden walnut! She broke it open and found it was full of precious jewels.

She knew all trolls are greedy, so she brought them to the troll princess and said, "All these I will give you if you put off the wedding one day and let me go into the bridegroom's chamber alone at night."

The troll princess agreed, but she gave the young knight a sleeping potion in the evening.

When the girl went into the room of her beloved, he was sleeping heavily, and she could not wake him. She spoke to him, called to him, and sang to him:

*The smith's forge I worked for thee,*
*The glassy hill I climbed for thee,*
*Thy bloody clothes I wrung for thee;*
*Will thou not waken and turn to me?*

But he slept on and did not waken. When dawn came, the girl left, and he never knew she had been there.

The next day her heart was full of grief. She broke open the golden hickory nut, and the jewels inside were more brilliant than the others. So again she offered the rich jewels to the greedy troll princess, if she would put off the wedding one more day and allow her to stay the night in the room where the young man slept. But again the troll princess gave the knight a sleeping potion.

Again the girl tried to wake him. She called to him and she sang to him:

*The smith's forge I worked for thee,*
*The glassy hill I climbed for thee,*
*Thy bloody clothes I wrung for thee;*
*Will thou not waken and turn to me?*

But he slept heavily until morning and never knew she had been there.

The girl felt her heart would break. She had only the hazelnut left, so she opened it, and inside were the most brilliant jewels of all. When she showed these jewels to the troll princess, the princess could not resist them. She agreed to allow the girl in the room one last night.

Now it happened that the same day, the young man overheard two troll servants talking together about the strange sighs and singing in the captive knight's chamber. The young man resolved to stay awake that night to see who came into his room. He suspected that the posset he was given to drink that evening was a sleeping potion, and he secretly poured it away.

This time the girl found the young knight wide awake when she entered his room. He recognized her at once, and as soon as they embraced each other, the trolls' spell was broken—finally and completely.

While all around them slept, they silently left

the house and hurried away from the land of the trolls. They slid down the glass hill and made their way back to their own country.

And there, in a fine castle of their own, they lived in peace and contentment ever after.

*Different versions of this tale exist in England. It has Norse elements—the eerie blue light, the glass hill—and is believed to be very old. This retelling by the editor uses* **JOSEPH JACOBS** *and* **FLORA ANNIE STEELE** *as sources.*

**L**ong, long ago there was a caterpillar as fat as an elephant. His mouth was as red as his tail. His body was covered with hair and on his head was a long pointed horn.

One day, Mory, Bamba, and Badjina went to the field. On the way, they met the caterpillar, who had spread himself across the road to sleep. The children could not pass.

Bamba, who was very well-behaved, greeted him politely, saying, "Good day, Papa."

"M'ba,"* answered the caterpillar and moved aside to let him pass.

Next Mory spoke to him. "Good day, Grandfather. How are you?"

---

*Good day, thank you.

"M'ba," replied the caterpillar and little Mory got his turn to pass.

Then Badjina came forward. He wanted to pass too but he was not a well-behaved boy. He was not polite like his friends. He approached the caterpillar and shouted, "Good day, caterpillar." The caterpillar did not answer. He remained as he was, blocking the road with his long, furry body.

Badjina yelled once more, "Red-mouthed caterpillar, I said good day."

The caterpillar did not answer. He did not budge. Badjina screamed, "Red-tailed caterpillar, I said good day."

At last the caterpillar, looking a little redder than usual, got really angry and *HOP!!!!* He swallowed Badjina in one gulp.

Mory and Bamba were very frightened. They hid in the bush and only when the caterpillar was out of sight did they dare to return to the village.

Badjina's father ran to the chieftain. "My son has been eaten by a fat caterpillar!" he moaned.

The chieftain called all the men together. "Bring your guns," he ordered, "all your arrows, your bows. We must find the caterpillar, and when we do, we shall kill him."

The men scurried into the bush. But when they

caught sight of the huge caterpillar, when they saw his gigantic red mouth and the long pointed horn on his head, they turned tail, threw away their guns, and rushed headlong to the village without once looking back.

"Why are you running? Where is my son? What's going on?" asked Badjina's mama.

"You couldn't begin to know," answered the chieftain. "That animal is as fat as the 'baobab* de Diamadougou.' His mouth is bigger than a calabash. We are afraid and we are running to save ourselves."

Badjina's mother cried and cried, but the oldest woman of the village comforted her, saying, "Inasmuch as the men can't bring Badjina to you, we women shall go and kill the caterpillar. We shall bring your child home to you."

Quickly the women formed a group. Some carried sticks that pound grain, some brought big wooden cooking spoons, some brought knives that they used to peel yams, and others even brought hatchets with which they cut firewood.

As they left the village they made fun of the men. "We women aren't afraid," they said. "We shall

---

*The baobab is a large tree native to tropical Africa. It has an exceedingly thick trunk and bears a gourdlike fruit.

bring back the red tail of the caterpillar and the big pointed horn from his head."

After walking for several hours the women found the caterpillar. He was, as always, in the middle of the road. He slept just like a boa constrictor ready to swallow a hind.

Bindou, the most courageous of the women, approached the caterpillar on tiptoe. She took one step, two steps, three steps until she was almost on top of the animal. Then she raised her grain-pounding stick very high, then higher, and even higher and . . . *pow!* . . . with one tremendous whack she finished him off. "Everybody, everybody come. Come quickly!" she shouted.

The women came running . . . *thump!* . . . *thump!* . . . *thump!*

"The caterpillar is dead!" they shrilled with excitement. "Let us open the belly quickly."

And do you know what they found? Little Badjina, alive and unharmed.

The women cut strong vines from the bushes and tied the caterpillar up. Then they dragged the animal back to the village.

"Look, look," they called, "we have found Badjina and he is alive. We women have killed the caterpillar."

"Cut him up in bits," cried all the others.

Alas, with each cut of the knife, ten, a hundred, a thousand little caterpillars issued forth from the body of the fat animal. They crawled on the ground in the streets in the village square and even in the houses.

And that is why, even today, we find caterpillars everywhere on the earth.

*This story from the Côte d'Ivoire was told by* **WILLIAM KAUFMAN** *in the* Unicef Book of Children's Legends *(1970).*

# The LAIRD'S LASS and the GOBHA'S SON

An old laird had a young daughter once, and she was the pawkiest lass in all the world. Her father petted her and her mother cosseted her till the wonder of it was that she wasn't so spoiled that she couldn't be borne. What saved her was that she was so sunny and sweet by nature, and she had a merry way about her that won all hearts. Nonetheless, when she set her heart on something she'd not give up till she got what she wanted.

Nobody minded so much while she was a wee thing, but when she was getting to be a young lady, that's when the trouble began.

She turned out better than anyone would have expected, considering all. You wouldn't have found a bonnier lass if you searched far and wide. But she was as stubborn as ever about having her own way.

Well, now that she was old enough the laird decided it was time to be finding a proper husband for her to wed, so he and her mother began to look about for a suitable lad.

It didn't take long for the lass to find out what they had in mind. She began to do a bit of looking around on her own. She hadn't the shade of a bit of luck at first. All the men who came to the castle were too fat or too thin or too short or too tall or else they were wed already. But she kept on looking just the same.

It was a good thing for her that she did, because one day, as she stood at the window of her bedroom, she saw the lad she could fancy in the courtyard below.

She called to her maid, "Come quick to the window! Who is the lad down below?"

The maid came and looked. "Och, 'tis only the son of the gobha* that keeps the shop in the village. No doubt the laird sent for him about shoeing the new mare," she said. And she went back to her work.

"How does it come that I ne'er saw him before?" asked the lass.

"The gobha's shop is not a place a young lady would be going to at all. Come away from the window now! Your mother would be in a fine fret could she see you acting so bold."

*A gobha is a blacksmith.

And no doubt she was right, for the lass was hanging over the windowsill.

The lass came away as she was told, but she had made up her mind to go down to the village and get another look at the gobha's son.

She liked the jaunty swing to his kilt, and she liked the way his yellow hair swept back from his brow, and she had a good idea there'd be a lot of other things about him she'd be liking, could she be where she could get a better look at him.

She knew she wouldn't be let go if she asked, so she just went without asking. And to make sure nobody'd know her, she borrowed the dairymaid's Sunday frock and bonnet. She didn't ask for the loan of them either, but just took them away when nobody was around to see.

The gobha's shop was a dark old place, but it wasn't so dark that she couldn't see the gobha's son shoeing the laird's new mare.

His coat was off and his arms were bare and he had a great smudge of soot on his cheek, but she liked what she saw of him even better than before.

He was holding the mare's leg between his knees and fixing the new shoe on its hoof, so she waited till he finished. Then she stepped inside.

"Good day," said she.

"Good day," said he, looking up in surprise. And

he gave her a wide smile that fair turned her heart upside down.

So she gave him one as good in return. "I'm from the castle," said she. "I just stopped in as I passed by to see how you were coming on with the mare."

"I've two shoes on and two to go," said he. "Bide here a bit and I'll ride you up on her back when I'm done."

"Och, nay!" said the laird's daughter. "I just stopped by. They'll be in a taking if I'm late coming home."

Though he begged her to stay, she would not. So off she went.

He was not well pleased to see her go for he'd taken a terrible fancy to her and wanted to know her better. It was only after she was gone that he remembered he'd never asked her name.

When he took the mare back, he tried to find out which of the maids from the castle had been in the village that day. But there were maids galore in the castle and half a dozen or more had been in the village on one errand or another, so he got no satisfaction. He had to go home and hope he'd be seeing her soon again. Whoever she was and wherever she was, she'd taken his heart along with her.

The laird's daughter had come home and put the dairymaid's frock and bonnet back where she got them. After she made herself tidy, she went to find her father. She found him with her mother in the second-best parlor and she stood before them and said, "You can just stop looking for a husband for me to wed because I've found the one I want myself."

The laird laughed, for he thought it a joke she was making, but he soon found out it was not.

"I'm going to marry the gobha's son!" said she.

The laird flew into a terrible rage. But no matter what he said, it was all of no use. The lass had made up her mind, and he couldn't change it for her. And it was no use bothering the gobha's son about it, because he didn't even know who she was. He'd just tell the laird he'd never laid eyes on his daughter.

Well, the laird could only sputter and swear, and his lady could only sit and cry, and the lass was sent to bed without her supper. But the cook smuggled it up to her on a tray, so that did her no harm at all.

The next morning the laird told her that she and her mother were going to Edinburgh in a week's time. And there she'd stay until she was safely wed to her second cousin twice removed whom he'd finally picked to be her husband. The cousin had asked for her hand before, but the laird had been putting him off in case someone better came along.

But the way things were, the laird had decided he'd better take the cousin after all, and get his daughter wed to a husband her mother and he had picked for her themselves.

"I'll go if I must," said the lass. "But you can tell my cousin that I'll not be marrying him. I've made up my mind to wed the gobha's son!"

The gobha's son was having his own troubles.

When the laird and his family came out of the church on the Sabbath morn, they passed by the gobha and his son at the gate. When they'd gone by, the gobha's son pulled at his father's arm.

"Who is the lass with the laird and his lady?" he asked his father.

His father turned and looked. "Och, you ninny!" said he in disgust. "Can you not see 'tis no lass at all? 'Tis a young lady, so it is! That's the laird's own daughter."

The gobha's son had been building cloud castles about the lass he'd thought was one of the castle maids, and now they all tumbled down. His heart was broken because he was so unlucky as to fall in love with the daughter of the laird.

Well, the days went by till it came to the one before the lass and her mother were to go to Edinburgh. The lass rose from her bed at break of dawn and dressed herself and tiptoed down the stairs.

Since this was going to be her last day at home, she wanted to have a little time to be alone for it seemed that either the laird or her mother or else her maid was at her elbow ever since she'd told them she meant to wed the gobha's son.

The cook was in the kitchen as she passed through to the back of the castle. The cook was picking something up from the floor.

"What have you there?" asked the lass.

"'Tis a bairn's wee shoe," said the cook. "One of the laird's dogs fetched it in and dropped it on the floor just now as he went through. It must belong to one of the gardener's weans. 'Tis a bonny wee shoe and much too good for the likes of them," she added with a sniff.

"Give it to me," said the lass. "I'll find the bairn that owns it." She took the shoe and dropped it in her pocket.

Around the stables she went, and through the kitchen garden to the lane that led to the gardener's house. Halfway there she came upon a wee old man sitting on the bank at the side of the lane with his head in his hands. He was crying as if his heart would break. He was the smallest manikin ever she'd seen. He was no bigger than a bairn and indeed he looked so like a bairn, sitting there and weeping so sorely, that she sat down beside him and put her arms about him to comfort him. "Do not greet so sore," said she. "Tell me your trouble and if I can I'll mend it."

"'Tis my shoe!" wept the wee man. "I took it off to take out a stone that got in it, and a great rough dog snatched it from my hand and ran off with it. I cannot walk o'er the briers and brambles and the cruel sharp stones without my shoes and I'll ne'er get home today."

"Well now!" said the lass, with a laugh. "It seems I can mend your troubles easier than my own. Is this what you're weeping for?" And she put her hand in her pocket and took out the shoe she had taken from the cook.

"Och, aye!" cried the wee man. "'Tis my bonny wee shoe!" He caught it from her hand and put it on and, springing into the road, he danced for joy. But in a minute he was back, sitting on the bank beside her.

"Turnabout is only fair," said he. "What are your troubles? Happen I can mend them as you did mine."

"Mine are past mending," said the lass. "For they're taking me to Edinburgh in the morn, to wed my second cousin twice removed. But I'll not do it. If I can't marry the gobha's son, I'll marry no man at all. I'll lay down and die before I wed another!"

"Och, aye!" said the wee man thoughtfully. "So you want to marry the gobha's son. Does the gobha's son want to wed you?"

"He would if he knew me better," the lass said.

"I could help you," the manikin told her, "but you might have to put up with a bit of inconvenience. You mightn't like it."

"Then I'll thole* it," the lass said. "I'd not be minding anything if it came right for me in the end."

"Remember that," said the wee man laughing, "when the right time comes."

Then he gave her two small things that looked like rowan berries, and told her to swallow them before she slept that night.

"You can leave the rest to me," said he with a grin. "You'll not be going to Edinburgh in the morn!"

When the night came, what with packing and getting ready for the next day's journey, all in the castle went to bed early, being tired out. The laird locked the door of his daughter's room lest the lass take it into her head to run away during the night.

*To thole is to endure.

Early the next morn, the maid came up with the lass's breakfast tray. Since the door was locked, she had to put the tray down and go fetch the key from the laird's room.

"I'll come with you," the lass's mother said to the maid. So she got the key from under the laird's pillow and unlocked the lass's door. When she opened the door and went in, she screamed and fainted away. The maid behind her looked to see why, and the tray dropped out of her hands. The laird heard the racket and came running. He rushed into the room, and there was his wife on the floor, and the maid, with the tray and the dishes and all at her feet, wringing her hands. He looked at the bed. His daughter wasn't there!

"She's flummoxed us!" said the laird. "Where can she have gone to!"

He and the maid got the laird's wife into a chair and brought her to. The first thing she said was, "Have you looked at the bed?"

"I have!" said the laird grimly. "The pawky lass! She's got away. The bed's empty."

"My love," said his wife weakly. " 'Tis not empty."

The laird went over to the bed and his lady came with him. The bed was not empty, though his daughter was not in it.

In her place, with its head on the pillow and its

forelegs on the silken coverlet, lay a wee white dog!

"What is that dog doing in my daughter's bed?" shouted the laird. "Put the beastie out in the hall at once!" And he made to do it himself. But his wife caught his arm.

"I do not think it is a dog," she said. "I very much fear the wee dog is our daughter."

"Havers!" the laird said angrily. "Have you all gone daft?"

But they pointed out to him that the doggie was wearing the blue silk nightgown that her mother's  own hands had put on her daughter last night. And hadn't the maid braided her young lady's hair and tied it with a blue satin ribbon? Well then, to look at the wee dog's forelock all braided and tied the same, 'twas plain to see that someone had put a spell on the lass and turned her into a dog.

"Nonsense!" said the laird in a rage. "Are you telling me I do not know my daughter from a dog?" And he strode over to the bed. But when he leaned over to pluck the animal from the covers, it looked up at him. The laird looked back in horror, for he saw that the eyes were his daughter's own, and the grin on its face was uncommonly like his lass's own wide naughty smile. And around its neck was the golden chain with the locket he'd given her long ago that she'd worn since he put it there.

But the laird would not admit it. 'Twas all a trick! So he made them search the room from corner to corner and in every cupboard and press. He looked up the chimney himself and got himself covered with smuts, but all he saw was the blue sky above the chimney pot. She was not in the room. She couldn't have got out the windows. She couldn't have gone through the door, for he'd had the key to it. So it all came to this—the wee dog in the bed was his daughter.

He went over to have another look and as he bent down, the little dog chuckled with his daughter's own pleased chuckle and patted him on the cheek just as his daughter used to do. That settled it.

"Och, you wee rascal!" said the laird, never being able to find it in his heart to be angry with his daughter. "Now what are we to do?" There was one thing that was certain and sure. They'd not be going to Edinburgh that day. So a messenger was sent to the second cousin twice removed, to tell him that he needn't be expecting them. The servants were told the lass was down in bed with some sort of an illness, and nobody but her maid was to come into the room lest they catch it. That was enough to keep them all away.

The laird had his own physician come from Edinburgh though his wife told him 'twould do no good at all. He made the man promise not to tell what he saw, then took him into his daughter's room. The doctor looked and shook his head. Then he looked at the dog again and rubbed his eyes. "'Tis strange!" he muttered. "I do not see a young lady. I see naught but a wee white dog."

"You see a dog because there is a dog!" shouted the laird.

"'Tis an optical delusion! Begging your lairdship's pardon, your lairdship's daughter is not a dog," insisted the doctor.

"'Tis my daughter," the laird roared. "And she is a dog. So be off with you!"

Well, the maid and his wife were right. The doctor was no use at all. He went back to Edinburgh and wrote a learned paper called "Remarkable Manifestation of Hallucination in A__shire," which was read by learned societies all over the world, but didn't help the laird at all.

Then the maid suggested they send for an old wife she'd heard of. The old woman came with herbs and powders, but all she could do was tell them the lass had been bewitched. How to take the spell off, she didn't know at all.

The laird was fair distracted, her ladyship took to her bed, and the maid went about in tears from morn till night. All the servants in the castle said it must be a mortal illness the young lady had on her, and they tippy-toed and grieved as they went about their work.

The maids carried the news to the village, and the gobha's son soon heard all about it. If he thought his heart was broken before, it was twice as bad when he thought the laird's daughter might be about to die. For if she were living, at least he'd have a chance to lay his eyes on her now and again. He felt he couldn't be expected to bear it.

He was hammering away at a bit of metal his father had told him to make a brace of, not even noticing the iron had gone cold, when a shadow fell across the door. He looked up and there was the strangest sight he'd ever seen in his life. A wee bit of a man was there all dressed in green from his neck to his heels, and his shoes and his cap were red. He was mounted on a horse so small it could have stood under the belly of any horse the gobha's son had ever seen before, but it was the right size for the wee man in green.

The gobha's son stared, while the wee man got down from his horse and led it into the shop.

"Gobha," said the wee man. "Can you shoe my horse?"

"I'm not the gobha," said the lad. "I'm the gobha's

son, and I can shoe your horse. 'Twill take me a while, for I've ne'er shod a beast so small before and I've no notion of the size the shoes must be."

" 'Tis no matter," said the wee man. "I've time galore. I'll sit and gab a bit with you till the task is done."

So he made himself comfortable in a corner beyond the forge, and crossing his knees with an easy air, he started to talk to the gobha's son.

It was plain to see that the lad was in no mood for talking. The wee man said the weather had been fine for the time of the year. The lad said only, "Aye. Is it?"

Then the man in green said the fishing was good, he'd heard. To that the lad said happen it was. He wouldn't be knowing.

Then the manikin tried him on the fair in the market town over the hill, but the gobha's son only sighed and said nothing at all.

It was taking a long time, as he said it would, for the horse's hooves were small beyond believing. Shoe after shoe had to be thrown back because they were all too big. But at last he got a set that would fit, and putting the horse where the light fell best, he started to put the horseshoes on its feet.

"I'll get you talking yet, my lad," the wee man said to himself.

So, when the gobha's son started to put the shoe on the wee nag's foot, the manikin said, "Have you e'er seen the bonny daughter of the laird up at the castle?"

The gobha's son jumped as if he'd been stuck with a pin. But all he said was, "Aye."

The wee man waited until the lad finished putting the first shoe on. When he picked up the second leg and started to fix the second shoe to the hoof, the wee man asked, "Has anyone told you that she's mortal ill?"

The gobha's son gave a great big sigh, but all he said was, "Aye."

He finished with that shoe and went around to the other side of the wee horse. When he looked to be well started on the third shoe, the man in green asked, "Have you not been up to the castle to ask about the laird's bonny daughter?"

The gobha's son shot him a glowering look. "Nay," said he.

That took care of the chatting between the two until the horse was nearly shod. As he was about to fix the last nail in the last of the shoes, the man in green said, "Would you be knowing what ails the bonny young lady?"

The gobha's son waited until he had finished

his work and the horse stood with shoes on all four feet. Then he turned to the wee man and he said, "Nay!" He threw the hammer he'd been using aside and told the wee man, "There's your horse all shod and well shod. Now will you take it and yourself away and leave me in peace?"

The wee man stayed where he was. "Not yet!" said he with a grin. "Why do you not go up to the castle and cure the laird's bonny daughter yourself?"

"Cure her!" shouted the gobha's son. "I'd lay down my life to cure her, the bonny young thing." And he asked the wee man furiously, "How could the likes of me do any good when they've had the old wife with her herbs and simples, and the best physician come all the way from Edinburgh, and neither of them could set her on her feet again?"

"Whisht, lad!" the manikin scolded. "Would you have all the village running to see what the matter can be? To be sure, they couldn't help her. But I know a way you could cure her. If you'd want to."

As soon as the gobha's son heard that, he was at the wee man to tell him, so that he could run to the castle at once and cure the laird's daughter of her illness.

"Answer me this first," the green manikin said. "Would you like to wed the bonny young lady?"

"Are you daft?" groaned the lad. "Who ever heard of a gobha's son wedding the daughter of a laird?"

"'Tis not what I asked you," said the wee man. "Look, lad! Would you like to wed her?"

"Before I'd wed with anyone else, I'd just lay down and die!" cried the gobha's son.

"'Tis just what the laird's daughter said about yourself," said the wee man with a satisfied grin. "So, since you are both of the same mind, I'll help you!" Then the wee green man told the gobha's son what he and the lass had been up to.

"Och, nay!" said the lad. "'Tis beyond believing."

"It all started because she made up her mind to wed the gobha's son," said the manikin. "So let's you and me be finishing it!"

The wee man gave him two wee things, like rowan berries, as like the ones he'd given the lass as they could be.

"Here's the cure for what ails her," he told the gobha's son.

The lad was all for rushing off to the castle at once, but the wee man held him back.

"Will you be going up to the castle the way you are with your leather apron and soot from the forge all over you?" he scolded. "Och, they'd run you off the place e'er you got the first word in. Tidy yourself first, lad!"

So the lad went and cleaned himself up and got into his Sunday clothes, and a fine figure he was, to be sure. 'Twas no wonder the laird's daughter had set her heart upon him!

"Go with my blessing," said the wee man. "But remember! Don't cure the lass till the laird has given his promise that you can wed her."

"That I'll not!" said the gobha's son. He squared his shoulders, and off he marched to the castle.

The wee man got on his wee horse's back and where he rode to, nobody knows.

Things at the castle were in a terrible state. The laird was at his wit's end. The laird's wife and the castle servants had wept till the walls were damp with the moisture from their tears. The laird's daughter was getting tired of being a dog, and beginning to fear that she'd ne'er be anything else for the rest of her life. She had snapped at the laird's hand that morning because she was cross with him for not letting her wed the gobha's son in the first place. 'Twas a weary day for the old laird.

The gobha's son walked up to the front door and asked to see the laird. He had such a masterful way with him the servants let him in at once, and in no time at all there he was, face to face with the laird.

The laird had left his manners off for the time. "Well who are you and what do you want?" he asked with a frown.

"I'm the gobha's son," said the lad. When the laird heard who it was, he jumped from his chair and started for the lad, ready to throw him out with his own two hands. Because it was the gobha's son who was at the bottom of all the trouble.

The gobha's son sidestepped the laird and said quickly, "And I've come to cure your daughter."

Och, now! That made a difference. Where the laird had been all wrath and scowls, he was now all smiles. He caught the lad by the arm and said, "A hundred thousand welcomes! Come, let's be going to her then."

"Nay," said the lad. "I must know first what I'll get for it."

"Do not let that fash you," the laird said eagerly. "Och, I'll give you a whole big bag of gold. Or two if you like. Come. Let's be at it!"

"'Tis not gold I want," said the lad.

"What is it, then?" the laird asked impatiently.

"Your leave to marry your daughter," said the lad as bold as brass.

"Nay!" thundered the laird. "That you shan't have."

"Then I'll bid you good day," said the gobha's son, and started for the door.

But he never got there. The laird was beside him before he laid his hand on the door knob.

What could the poor old laird do? He had to give in and he knew it. So he did.

"You can have her," said the laird to the gobha's son.

The wee dog jumped from the bed and ran up to the gobha's son the minute he and the laird came into the room. The lad took the berries from his pocket and popped them into her mouth and she swallowed them down. Before you could say, "Two twos," there stood the laird's daughter in the wee dog's place!

She took the lad's hand in her own and she turned to the laird and said, "I'm going to wed the gobha's son."

"Wed him then!" said the laird, not too unhappy about it since he'd got his lass back again. "But you'd better go tell your mother and the maids, so they can stop crying if you want the castle dried out by the time of your wedding."

So the pawky lass got her way in the end and married the gobha's son. The laird was not ill pleased for he found his son-in-law as likeable a body as any he'd ever found. He made him steward of his estates and a good one the lad was, too. So it all ended well and that's all there is to tell about the laird's daughter and the gobha's son.

*"Wee Man"* is one of the names given to the smaller Celtic fairies—the pixies, leprechauns, and hobgoblins. They are inclined to be friendly to humans and to repay favors. This is reprinted from Thistle and Thyme *(1962)* by **SORCHE NIC LEODHAS**.

Once upon a time there was an old woman who lived by herself on the edge of the great wild moor. Many tales the folk thereabouts told of fiends, spirits, and all manner of fearful things that roamed the moor at night. You may be sure they took care never to be abroad on that bleak stretch of lonely land once darkness had fallen.

Now it happened the old woman had to cross the moor once a week to reach the market town to sell her butter and eggs. She usually rose early, just before dawn, to set out. One night, knowing the next day to be market day, she went to bed quite early. When she awoke, she began to get ready for her journey. It was still dark of course, and, having no clock, she did not know it was still before midnight. She dressed, ate, saddled her horse, and attached to it the large wicker panniers containing the butter and eggs. Wrapping a worn old cloak about her, she and the horse sleepily set off across the moor.

She had not gone very far before she heard the sounds of a pack of hounds baying under the stars and saw, racing toward her, a white hare. When it reached her, the hare leapt up on a large rock close by the path as if to say, "Come, catch me."

The old woman chuckled. She liked the idea of outwitting the hounds, so she reached out her hand, picked up the crouching hare, and popped it into one of her wicker panniers. She dropped the lid and rode on.

The baying of the hounds came nearer, and suddenly she saw a headless horse galloping toward her, surrounded by a pack of monstrous hounds. On the horse sat a dark figure with horns sprouting out of his head. The eyes of the hounds shone fiery red, while their tails glowed with a blue flame.

It was a terrifying sight to behold. Her horse stood trembling and shaking, but the woman sat up boldly to confront the horned demon. She had the hare in her basket and didn't intend to give it up. But it seemed that these monstrous creatures were not very clever or knowing, for the rider asked the old woman, very civilly, had she seen a white hare run past and did she know in which direction it had gone.

"No indeed," she said firmly. "I saw no hare run past me." Which of course was true.

The rider spurred his headless horse, called his hounds to follow, and galloped across the moors. When they were out of sight, the woman patted and calmed her shivering horse.

Suddenly, to her surprise, the lid of the pannier moved and then opened. It was no frightened hare who came forth, but a woman all in white.

The ghostly lady spoke in a clear voice. "Dame," she said, "I admire your courage. You have saved me from a terrible enchantment and now the spell is broken. I am no human woman—it was my fate to be condemned for centuries to the form of a hare and to be pursued on the moor at night by evil demons, until I could get behind their tails while they passed on in search of me. Through your courage the enchantment is broken, and I can now return to my own kind. We will never forget you. I promise that all your hens shall lay two eggs instead of one, your cows shall give plenty of milk year round, your garden crops shall thrive and yield a fine harvest. But beware the devil fiend and his evil spirits, for he will try to do you harm once he realizes you were clever enough to outwit him. May good fortune attend you."

The mysterious lady vanished and was never seen again, but all she promised came true. The woman had the best possible luck at market that morning and continued to have good fortune with all her crops and livestock. The devil never did succeed in getting revenge—though he had many a try—and the kindly protection of the ghostly lady stayed with the woman the rest of her life.

*Originally, "White Ladies" were early pagan deities who gave fertility to land and livestock; now they are thought of as Celtic ghosts or fairies. Headless horses and monstrous, baying hounds appear in folktales from the southwest of England and were used by Sir Arthur Conan Doyle in his* Hound of the Baskervilles. *The editor's source for this retelling was* **EDWIN SIDNEY HARTLAND***'s* English Fairy and Folk Tales *(1890).*

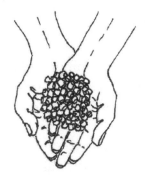

**T**here once was a rich farmer who was as grasping and mean as he was rich. He was always driving a hard bargain and always getting the better of his poor neighbors. One of these neighbors was a humble shepherd to whom the farmer owed payment of a calf. When the time of payment came, the farmer refused to give the shepherd the calf, forcing the shepherd to bring the matter to the burgomaster* of the village.

The burgomaster was a young man who was not very experienced. He listened to both sides, and when he had thought a bit, he said, "Instead of making a decision on this case, I will put a riddle to you both, and the man who makes the best answer shall have the calf. Are you agreed?"

*A burgomaster is the mayor of a village.

The farmer and the shepherd accepted this proposal, and the burgomaster said, "Well then, here is my riddle: What is the swiftest thing in the world? What is the sweetest thing? What is the richest? Think out your answers and bring them to me at this same time tomorrow."

The farmer went home in a temper. "What kind of a burgomaster is this young fellow!" he growled. "If he had let me keep the calf, I'd have sent him a bushel of pears. Now I may lose the calf, for I can't think of an answer to his foolish riddle."

"What is the riddle?" asked his wife. "Perhaps I can help you." The farmer told her the riddle, and his wife said that of course she knew the answers.

"Our gray mare must be the swiftest thing in the world," said she. "You know that nothing ever passes us on the road. As for the sweetest, did you ever taste any honey sweeter than ours? And I'm sure there's nothing richer than our chest of golden ducats that we've saved up over the years."

The farmer was delighted. "You're right! Now we will be able to keep the calf!"

Meanwhile, when the shepherd got home, he was very downcast and sad. His daughter, a clever girl named Manka, asked what troubled him.

The shepherd sighed. "I'm afraid I've lost the calf. The burgomaster gave us a riddle to solve, and I know I shall never guess it."

"What is the riddle? Perhaps I can help you," said Manka.

The shepherd told her the riddle, and the next day, as he was setting out for the burgomaster's, Manka told him the answers.

When the shepherd reached the burgomaster's house, the farmer was already there. The burgomaster repeated the riddle and then asked the farmer his answers.

The farmer said with a pompous air: "The swiftest thing in the world? Why that's my gray mare, of course, for no other horse ever passes us on the road. The sweetest? Honey from my beehives. The richest? What can be richer than my chest of gold pieces?"

"Hmmm," said the burgomaster. "And what answers does the shepherd make?"

"The swiftest thing in the world," said the shepherd, "is thought, for thought can run any distance in the twinkling of an eye. The sweetest thing of all is sleep, for when a person is tired and sad, what can be sweeter? The richest thing is the earth, for out of the earth come all the riches of the world."

"Good!" cried the burgomaster. "The calf goes to the shepherd."

Later the burgomaster said to the shepherd, "Tell me now, who gave you those answers? I'm sure you never thought of them yourself."

The shepherd was unwilling to tell, but finally he confessed that the answers came from his daughter, Manka. The burgomaster became very interested in the cleverness of Manka, and he sent his housekeeper for ten eggs and gave them to the shepherd.

"Take these eggs to Manka and tell her to have them hatched by tomorrow and bring me the chicks," said he.

The shepherd went home and gave Manka the eggs and the message. Manka laughed and said, "Take a handful of corn and bring it back to the burgomaster with this message, "My daughter says if you plant this corn, grow it, and have it harvested by tomorrow, she will bring you the ten chicks to feed on your ripe grain."

When the burgomaster heard this answer, he laughed heartily. "That's a very clever daughter you have! I'd like to meet her. Tell her to come to see me, but she must come neither by day nor by night, neither riding nor walking, neither dressed nor undressed."

Manka smiled when she received this message. The next dawn, when night was gone and day not yet arrived, she set out. She had wrapped herself in a fishnet, and throwing one leg over a goat's back and keeping one foot on the ground, she went to the burgomaster's house.

Now I ask you, did she go dressed? No, she wasn't dressed, for a fishnet isn't clothing. Did she go undressed? Of course not, for wasn't she covered with a fishnet? Did she walk to the burgomaster's? No, she didn't walk, for she went with one leg thrown over a goat. Then did she ride? Of course she didn't ride, for wasn't she walking on one foot?

When she reached the burgomaster's house, she called out, "Here I am, and I've come neither by day nor by night, neither riding nor walking, neither dressed nor undressed."

The young burgomaster was so delighted with Manka's cleverness that he proposed to her, and in a short time they were married.

"But understand, my dear Manka," he said, "you are not to use your cleverness at my expense. You must not interfere in any of my cases. If you give advice to those who come to me for judgment, I'll send you home to your father!"

"Very well," said Manka. "I agree not to give advice in your cases unless you ask for it."

All went well for a time. Manka was busy with housekeeping, and was careful not to interfere in any of the burgomaster's cases.

Then one day two farmers came to the burgomaster to have a dispute settled. One of the farmers owned a mare which had foaled in the marketplace. The colt had run under the wagon of the other farmer, and the owner of the wagon claimed the colt as his property.

The burgomaster was thinking of something else while the case was being argued, and he said carelessly, "The man who found the colt under his wagon is the owner of the colt."

The farmer who owned the mare met Manka as he was leaving the house, and stopped to tell her about the case. Manka was ashamed that her husband had made so foolish a decision. She said to the farmer, "Come back this afternoon with a fishing net and stretch it across the dusty road. When the burgomaster sees you, he will come out and ask what you are doing. Tell him you are catching fish. When he asks how you can expect to catch fish in a dusty road, tell him it's just as easy to catch fish in a dusty road as it is for a wagon to foal a colt . . . He'll see the injustice of his decision and have the colt returned to you. But remember one thing—you must not let him know that I told you to do this."

That afternoon when the burgomaster looked out of his window, he saw a man stretching a fishnet across the dusty road. He went out and asked, "What are you doing?"

"Fishing."

"Fishing in a dusty road? Are you crazy?"

"Well," said the man, "it's just as easy for me to catch fish in a dusty road as it is for a wagon to foal."

Then the burgomaster realized he had made a careless and unjust decision. "Of course, the colt belongs to your mare and it must be returned to you," he said. "But tell me, who put you up to this? You didn't think of it yourself!"

The farmer tried not to tell, but the burgomaster persisted and when he found out that Manka was at the bottom of it he became very angry. He rushed into the house and called his wife.

"Manka," he said, "I told you what would happen if you interfered in any of my cases! I won't hear any excuses. Home you go this very day, and you may take with you the one thing you like best in the house."

Manka did not argue. "Very well, my dear husband. I shall go home to my father's cottage and take with me the one thing I like best in the house. But I will not go until after supper. We have been very happy together, and I should like to eat one last meal with you. Let us have no more angry words, but be kind to each other as we've always been, and then part as friends."

The burgomaster agreed to this, and Manka prepared a fine supper of all the dishes her husband particularly liked. The burgomaster opened his choicest wine and pledged Manka's health. Then he set to eat, and the supper was so good that he ate and ate and ate. And the more he ate, the more he drank, until at last he grew drowsy and fell sound asleep in his chair. Then, without awakening him, Manka had him carried out to the wagon that was waiting to take her home to her father.

The next morning when the burgomaster opened his eyes, he found himself lying in the shepherd's cottage.

"What does this mean?" he roared.

"Nothing, dear husband," said Manka. "You know you told me I might take with me the one thing I liked best in your house, so of course I took you! That's all."

The burgomaster stared at her in amazement. Then he laughed loud and heartily to think how Manka had outwitted him.

"Manka," he said, "you're too clever for me. Come, my dear, let's go home."

So they climbed back into the wagon and drove home.

The burgomaster never again scolded his wife, but after that, whenever a very difficult case came up, he always said, "I think we had better consult my wife. You know she's a very clever woman."

*Variations of this Central European story appear in different cultures and countries. "The Innkeeper's Daughter" is an exact parallel in Jewish folklore, while a similar tale, "The Basil Plant," is found in Chile. All folktales of this type turn on a woman's wise answers, usually to riddles. This retelling by the editor is taken from* **PARKER FILLMORE**'s *story in* Shoemaker's Apron *(1920).*

# NOTES ON THE TALES

**F**olktales are about human behavior in a world of magic and adventure. Underneath the entertainment of the surface story, there are usually one or more themes that illuminate the way the characters react, adding a deeper meaning to the tale. As noted in the preface, the tales teach moral and social values through the ways people deal with one another and the dilemmas that confront them.

## *Romantic Tales*
In "Janet and Tamlin" and "The Laird's Lass and the Gobha's Son," the heroines are not passive maidens awaiting the hero's choice. Both heroines actively make *their* choice of the loved one, and then overcome formidable obstacles and dangers to achieve their goals. Janet must wrest her lover from the Fairy Queen's power; the laird's

lass stands firm against an arranged marriage to win the husband of her choice.

## Tales of Magic and Enchantment

The theme of the young man, maiden, or child captured by the fairy host is an old one in Celtic folklore, and not all the tales end happily. A confrontation is usually required, and here Janet's courage is severely tested before she achieves her lover's freedom. The two tales also illustrate the differing attitudes of fairies and otherworld creatures; some are selfish or malevolent, others are disposed to be friendly and repay favors. That the laird's lass entrusts her life and fate to the wee man is an act of unusual courage.

In "The Black Bull of Norroway," the hero has been enchanted into an animal shape by supernatural forces of evil; he is doomed to exist in that shape until someone performs the specific rites which will break the enchantment and free him. The theme is, of course, familiar, but this heroine does not sit in luxurious passivity until the spell is broken, as the heroine does in "Beauty and the Beast." Instead, the girl looks beyond the animal form to the spirit within and actively sets about aiding the hero to break the enchantment.

The youngest sister in "The Black Bull of Norroway" does not yearn for a conventional marriage of status as her elder sisters do. The strangeness of a black bull as suitor does not daunt her and, moved by love and affection, she is determined to help him break the enchantment. The tasks and obstacles are difficult, but perseverance and self-discipline enable her to succeed. In this story, the hero's fate can only be resolved by the heroine's active help.

"Kate Crackernuts" is another tale of spells and enchantment, and, like the story of the Black Bull, has Norse and Celtic elements. It is actually an integration of two stories—the spell put upon Anne, Kate's beloved foster sister, and the enchantment of the prince. The strong affection between the sisters is unusual for fairy tales. This affection, and the animal-head spell cast over one sister, parallel the Norse tale "Tatterhood." In both tales it is the active, resourceful sister who takes determined steps to seek out the supernatural forces needed to break the enchantment. Kate also succeeds in freeing the young prince from his deadly enchantment, but this is not a tale of young lovers. Whether Kate eventually marries the prince is immaterial to the story's basic theme; Kate defeats the malevolent forces and receives recognition and reward.

## Tales of Relationships

Several of the tales concern couples and their interactions. The underlying themes emphasize the concept that mutual cooperation, as well as respect for each other's capabilities, are necessary to a couple's successful union.

In "The Prince and the Three Fates," a tale of the ancient Nile, the strength and determination of the princess enable her to save her husband's life. That she is instrumental in averting the doom predicted at his birth by fairies is unique—for most tales assume that the fate ordained by otherworld spirits cannot be changed. "My wife," says the prince, gratefully, "has been stronger than my fate." This is, in its way, a strongly positive theme, suggesting that the qualities and actions of human beings can alter and avert a fixed course of events. The princess is not a passive partner leaving the dilemma to her husband to solve; she takes decisive action to break the tragic prediction, and it is the prince's respect for his wife's capabilities that enables her to save him.

"What Happened to Six Wives Who Ate Onions" is a folktale built around a myth explaining the creation of star constellations. Anne Fisher, who adapted it for children, attributes the tale to the Western Mono Indians of California. Independent and strong-willed, the wives in this tale seek a new existence in the sky rather than submit to their husbands' ultimatum. A moral that may be

162

inferred from this marital conflict is that flexibility and compromise are necessary for the successful sharing of lives.

## Tales of Family and Community

Many tales deal with what could be called "family bonds" and, to some extent, a sense of community. In the African tale "Unanana and the Elephant," a mother's courage and cleverness bring about the rescue of her children. Unanana's feat takes on the nature of a "tall tale," for she sets free not only her own children, but a vast number of other people and animals devoured by the elephant. The element of community is echoed in "The Giant Caterpillar," a tale from Uganda. When one woman's child is devoured, all the women of the village band together to kill the monster; they rescue the child and rid the village of the menace permanently.

## Tales of Old Women

Two of the tales in the collection portray cheerful, capable old women. Endowed with practical wisdom and a sense of humor, they are remarkably unperturbed by the night demons they encounter. In "The Hedley Kow," the old woman is greatly entertained by the fearsome creature who has terrified the rest of the village folk. She accepts his changes of shape with good humor and acquires a companionable friend. The old farm woman of "The Hunted Hare" also lives alone, supporting herself with her livestock and crops. She meets the terrors of the monstrous hounds and headless horse with firmness, even defiance. The white hare, who is actually the enchanted White Lady, rewards her with abundance and prosperity. The women in both tales are attractive and spirited, a fine counterbalance to the negative images of hags and crones found in many other folk and fairy tales.

## Tales of Independent Women

Three generations of capable women turn up in the Japanese folktale "Three Strong Women." This nonsexist tale makes its point in a lighthearted manner. Tales of fantastic feats of strength are common in folklore, though few involve women. Although the story ends with the traditional rewards of gold and a desirable marriage, the elements that dominate the story are less familiar. Equality, mutual respect, and affection are evident in the relationship between the wrestler and the three women, as among the three women themselves. All four have expertise which they share with one another. The details of the ending take the theme of equality to its ultimate point, with delightful solemnity: the bride and groom take turns carrying each other up the hill. The strength of this tale lies in its clear affirmation of equality in relationships between people of different ages and sexes.

The Norse tale "Tatterhood" deals with themes of individuality and nonconformity. On the surface, it is a rollicking tale of twin sisters, opposite in nature, but very fond of one another. The calf's-head bewitchment of the gentle, docile sister is similar to the enchantment described in "Kate Crackernuts." In both cases, the aggressive sister effects the cure. But "Tatterhood" is primarily the story of an unconventional young personage, disdainful of approval, expected behavior, and pretty clothes. Her conception and birth are strange; from the beginning, there is a wild, elfin quality about her. She is endowed with unusual powers—but powers that are recognizably "good." Her mother, the queen, is pleased with the conventional twin, but throws up her hands in despair at Tatterhood. The king, however, seems to accept his daughter's strength and independence; he recognizes, when Tatterhood sets off with her sister for the outside world, that she is quite capable of sailing a ship unaided. Triumphing over wicked trolls, Tatterhood saves her sister and, in a distant land, meets a prince who appreciates her individuality.

The dialogue between the prince and Tatterhood that occurs at the end of the tale is a form of testing. Tatterhood, who, if she chooses, can transform her goat into a fine steed and her own appearance into a socially acceptable one, makes the point that she is also free to live her life as she chooses. When the prince recognizes and accepts Tatterhood's sovereignty over herself, he proves himself to be an acceptable partner.

"Tatterhood" is one of the most interesting folktales to come down to us. In the nineteenth century, Tatterhood was regarded as a social rebel, her behavior frowned upon. Her meek and mild, pretty twin sister was considered the ideal. In fact, the nineteenth-century folklorist who retold the tale called Tatterhood a "hussy." But it is clear that Tatterhood is the primary character and the true heroine of her adventures.

All the tales in this collection were chosen for their positive themes, as well as for their resourceful heroines. Bringing the underlying themes of these tales into sharper focus can give the adult reader a clearer insight into "messages" that are sometimes overlooked; the attitudes and values implicit in these stories from centuries past remain just as pertinent to our modern times.

# SUGGESTED READING

Favilli, Elena, and Francesca Cavallo. 2016. *Good Night Stories for Rebel Girls*. San Francisco: Timbuktu Labs.

Gaiman, Neil. 2015. *The Sleeper and the Spindle*. New York: HarperCollins.

Goble, Paul. 1993. *The Girl Who Loved Wild Horses*. New York: Aladdin.

Hamilton, Virginia. 1995. *Her Stories: African American Folktales, Fairy Tales, and True Tales*. New York: Blue Sky Press.

Lansky, Bruce. 2002. *The Best of Girls to the Rescue: Girls Save the Day*. Minnetonka, MN: Meadowbrook Press.

Martin, Rafe, and David Shannon. 1998. *The Rough-Face Girl*. New York: PaperStar Books.

McGoon, Greg. 2015. *The Royal Heart*. Lakewood, CA: Pelekinesis Publishing Group.

Ragan, Kathleen. 2000. *Fearless Girls, Wise Women, and Beloved Sisters: Heroines in Folktales from around the World*. New York: W. W. Norton & Company.

Sand, George. 2014. *What Flowers Say: And Other Stories*. Translated by Holly Erskine Hirko. New York: The Feminist Press.

Schatz, Kate. 2016. *Rad Women Worldwide*. Berkeley, CA: Ten Speed Press.

Yolen, Jane. 1986. *Favorite Folktales from around the World*. New York: Pantheon Books.

———. 2000. *Not One Damsel in Distress: World Folktales for Strong Girls*. Boston: Houghton Mifflin Harcourt.

# ACKNOWLEDGMENTS

My sincere thanks to local librarians, too numerous to name, in the Nassau County Library System and to librarians in the Donnell Children's Branch (New York Public Library) for their help and enthusiastic interest in my project. I also want to express my appreciation for the guidance and unfailing support given by my editors at the Feminist Press, Corrine B. Lucido and Sue Davidson.